Amy Peppercorn
## Out of Control

J Brindley lives with his partner in the south-east of England. He is keen on music of all different types, and enjoys playing squash and generally training to keep fit.

He has two children, a girl and a boy, both of whom have been instrumental in the development of his early stories for young people. He likes to draw ideas and inspiration from all aspects of life, especially from the people he meets. That's what happened when he met Amy Peppercorn.

**Why not contact Amy?**
**www.amypeppercorn.com**

**By the same author:**

Amy Peppercorn: Starry-eyed and Screaming
Amy Peppercorn: Living the Dream
Amy Peppercorn: Beyond the Stars
Changing Emma
Rhino Boy

# Amy Peppercorn
# Out of Control

## J Brindley

Orion
Children's Books

First published in Great Britain in 2006
by Orion Children's Books
a division of the Orion Publishing Group Ltd
Orion House
5 Upper Saint Martin's Lane
London WC2H 9EA

10 9 8 7 6 5 4 3 2 1

A catalogue record for this book is
available from the British Library.

Typeset at The Spartan Press Ltd,
Lymington, Hants

Printed in Great Britain by
Clays Ltd, St Ives plc

ISBN-10 1-84255-198-1
ISBN-13 978-1-84255-198-1

www.orionbooks.co.uk

 **One**

'**H**ello, Paris!' I screamed. 'Bonsoir!'

Paris screamed back at me.

'*Faire quelques bruit!*' I shouted into the mike, hoping that I'd got it somewhere near correct. '*Faire quelques bruit!*'

'Make some noise!'

Paris made some noise: a wonderful sound shouted back to me as I called out, 'I love your city!'

I did, too. It's a beautiful place, lively and stylish. They say Paris is romantic. It is! I'll tell you why . . .

Before I do, have you seen the video for my single, *Love Makes Me Sick*? That stuff we did when we filmed it a few months ago, dancing in Leicester Square with the street dancers and the drummers and the guitarist – the way that video cuts from the street at night to what looks like casual rehearsals in the studio – from there to footage of my fierce performance of the song on American TV. I like it so much!

Have you seen it? I hope you have. What I like about it is that it's real. There's nothing polished about it, nothing too over-the-top pop music business. That's what I like most, when I don't feel as if I'm being turned into a plastic model of what a pop star's supposed to look and sound and be like.

When we were filming, one of the street-dancers – and we used the real buskers and a real crowd; perhaps you were one of them? – came up to me and said, 'It must be really great being you.'

1

I'll never forget that. We were dancing together, and she was a better dancer than me, by far, but she wanted to let me know how great it must be just being me. I forget sometimes. I've had two Number One singles, a Number One album and I still keep forgetting how to relax and just enjoy myself.

Well, on stage in Paris, I remembered how great it was being me. 'Paris,' I called, sending out a shout to everyone in the whole city, and beyond, to all of France, to Germany, Spain, Belgium and the rest of Europe, during my first-ever starring gig in Europe, 'I love you!'

How could I possibly love everyone, a whole city full of people I'd never met? I can't answer that, because I don't know unless I'm on stage as I was then, calling out to a crowded auditorium and loving every second.

A few days before, I'd done a guest appearance in Hamburg, in Germany, at a concert given by Adam Bede, my – he was my friend. Becoming a really good friend, too. A French pop star, big all over Europe; all except the UK. It's not easy for a French singer, even one as big in Europe as Adam, to get a break in the UK. It's almost as difficult as an English girl like me making it in the States. But I wasn't doing too badly in France, and maybe soon in the rest of Europe. Adam Bede and his manager Pierre Piatta had been a great help here. My singles *If Ever* and *Proud* had been doing quite well in France and Belgium and Holland. These songs had been released through a French record label that Pierre Piatta was strongly connected with – he wasn't the owner, but had many shares in it and was a director of the company. Pierre was a great contact for my manager Raymond Raymond and his company Solar Records. They were talking about releasing an album in France next.

Here I was, doing a gig right in the heart of beautiful Paris, with my heart on my sleeve and my wings showing, singing, shouting out, screaming. The auditorium was fairly small and filled, I suspected, with many friends of Pierre Piatta and Adam Bede, other French singing artists under contract at Pierre Piatta Fantastique, PPF, members of the press, Solar people over from London, flown in especially to swell the numbers for my first French gig. Despite the fact that this wasn't a totally 'real' audience, in the truest sense I was flying high, loving it such a lot, giving it all I'd got.

For as long as I live I'll never get used to the feeling of performing live in this way with a live band, with my dear, sweet friend Lovely Leo on the keyboard. When my voice comes flying out, when I can use it to its full force, when I can move without trying, it's as if something else has taken control of my mind and body. I'm out of it, literally, rising above myself, seeing everything, feeling even more. There's nothing I can't do when I feel like this, running through all my old songs: *The Word on the Street, Proud, Love Makes Me Sick*.

And it gives me such a thrill!

'Make some noise!'

And then that wonderful, glorious sound came back: the massive, amassed voice of all who heard my cry and responded with one voice, which seemed never entirely disconnected from my own.

'Paris – you are beautiful!'

I ran from one side of the stage to the other. At least I think I did. One side of the stage one moment. 'Paris –' the other side a merest moment later '– you are beautiful!'

How such little legs as mine managed such breathtaking velocity I'll never know. There are many, many things I'll never know – like what the stuff is that replaces my blood when I feel like this. I think it must be helium, or laughing gas, or sheer adrenalin. Cut me, and I wouldn't bleed at all I bet – I'd go off *bang*, like a balloon at a fantastic champagne celebration party. I laughed.

'I can't tell you how good it is to be here. Can you all hear me?'

The audio system was so loud they could have heard me whispering. I screamed: 'Can you all hear me?'

A great cry came back. It was a scream. And it *was* great.

'I can't hear you!' I shrieked.

The sound that came back was like music; at least, it was to me. It was beautiful. Everyone in the whole auditorium must have called back to me.

'What?' I cried, leaning out from the front of the stage with one ear pushed forward with my hand funnelled round it. 'What did you say? You'll have to speak up. Make some noise!' I screamed.

They screamed. What a noise! It was beautiful. It said something, it really did. Don't ask me what, exactly, I couldn't say. But I could feel the meaning in it, as I could feel every meaning that could possibly have been said. It meant anything and everything – and I felt it all.

'I have a song,' I said, bringing the noise levels down a bit. 'This is a special song, given to me by a very special singer-songwriter. You might have heard of him? Adam Bede?'

Their applause, the claps and screams and whistles demonstrated their appreciation of even just Adam's name.

'This song is called *Never Let You Go*. I think it's very beautiful. I hope you think so too.'

Then I stood exactly where I was on the front of the stage, saying nothing, without moving, as the house lights went down and two spotlights picked me out as if I was entirely alone in the whole place. I wasn't. Adam had joined me, in the darkness to my left. We let a silence descend. When I say descend, that really is an accurate description, as any noise left over seemed to be forced to the ground and trodden down until we could hear nothing but the vague hum of the sound equipment. I waited, almost as if I could have picked the anticipation out of the air. Shivers were running up a thousand spines, I knew, because I could feel them, every one of them picking up the little hairs on the back of my neck. The whole place practically bristled with expectation. Only such a silence at exactly the right time can do this. I didn't do it alone; I can't make such a silence on my own. We all had to do it. We waited, we anticipated, we bristled.

I lifted a hand mike, breathing in deeply. Adam sang:

*I thought I saw you yesterday*

Another spotlight picked him out instantly. He looked – Adam has dark hair that falls over his collar, with even darker eyes. He has a look about him that makes me feel – but then, when that spotlight came on, the applause erupted for him so wildly we had to stop. We were looking, smiling at each other. Adam had given this song to me. It was beautiful. Quite sad, but very lovely. It was about loss: but whenever we sang it together, it was all about gain.

Adam started again:

*I thought I saw you yesterday*
*You looked how you looked*
*When you went away.*

I joined him:

*Nothing about you has changed*
*Though our lives have rearranged.*

He let me sing:

> *I think I see you everywhere,*
> *Same face, same smile,*
> *Same eyes, same hair,*
> *Exactly as you were before.*
> *We're not together any more.*

As the lyric said we were not together, we came together, walking to the centre of the stage as I sang that line, turning to sing together:

> *How can I forget you*
> *When you've never gone away from me?*

We looked at each other. Adam's dark eyes with the spot-lights shining into them were like beads of light themselves, glowing with inner force and energy.

I sang alone:

> *As I go on I cannot let you*
> *Age a day from me*

He sang:

> *The song of your voice, your breath in my hair,*
> *Your face in the new sunlight,*
> *My clothes, without yours, thrown over the chair.*

Together:

> *I reach for you in the night*

A ripple of applause rang round the auditorium. We went on, singing together, looking at each other:

*I saw you yesterday, today, I'll see you tomorrow,*
*You aren't there,*
*But I won't let you go.*
*Just cannot let you go!*

The song ended, but the instruments played on for a few bars. Adam was looking at me. I'd told my best friend Beccs I wasn't interested in Adam, not in that way. But he leaned forward and whispered in my ear. 'Just cannot let you go!'

The instrumental end to the song coincided with Adam kissing me. The audience applauded, shrieked, whistled as Adam kissed me on the lips. I'd told Beccs . . . but all the little hairs on the back of my neck were standing again, along with the audience as they applauded, shrieking and whistling as Adam kissed me.

And as I kissed him.

# ✳✳✳ TWO

'No, no,' Leo was enthusing, his hands flinging in every direction. 'I mean it. You were wonderful, wonderful! Both of you. My lovelies, when you two were on stage together, it was sheer – what was it? It was like *Breakfast at Tiffany's*. No – it was like *Brief Encounter*, only younger and with different accents.' He laughed.

Adam and I looked at each other.

'Oh, dear,' Lovely Leo said, catching our glance, 'you haven't the faintest idea, have you? Look, what I'm trying to say is that you two have something on stage individually; but together, it's more than multiplied. Do you follow me?'

'I think,' I said to Adam, 'that Leo's trying to say we looked good together.'

Adam went to speak.

Leo stopped him. 'Oh no, no! More, much more than that. There's some kind of magic to it. The way you sing together, the way it – it – it – Adam, I'm sure your lovely French language has a phrase for what I'm trying to say, doesn't it?'

'Only if Adam understands what you're trying to say,' I laughed.

'Oh,' Adam managed to say, 'I understand, totally. I know exactly. Maybe not the phrase, but I understand. I can – feel it. We are so good together, are we not?'

'You are.' Leo nodded. 'Everyone said so. Something special.'

We glanced at one another again. It was getting late. Leo was usually tucked up in bed long before now, even if he wouldn't have been asleep. I was waiting for him to leave to go back to our hotel. We'd been enjoying a very nice evening in a restaurant in Paris, Leo, Adam and me; but I wanted so much to talk to Adam without having my minder with me.

No, that's not fair. Leo wasn't a minder. Minders I'd had, on tour, in America: big bruisers in black suits with necks as wide as their heads and shoulders like American football players, which was something like rugby but with masses of padding. Leo, with his sparkly jumpers and slim slacks, could never be compared with those bouncers. But it was his job to look out for me, to get me safely from A to B on time, to ensure I got enough sleep and didn't eat only rubbish. Leo was lovely. I loved him. But sometimes, you know, it's like – well, it's like having your mum with you all the time. And sitting there in that beautiful café with Adam, of course I didn't want my mum or Leo around the whole time.

'Well,' Leo said, as if reading my mind, 'it's getting very late, isn't it?'

Both he and my mum seemed to be able to do that, to sometimes see what I was thinking. I had to hope Adam couldn't do it too. Every time I looked at him he made me think – actually, he stopped me thinking. There was something about the way he made me feel, both frightened and excited at the same time that stopped me thinking only of how dangerous it was for me to be around him.

Leo stretched and said, 'We should be getting back.' He was making a great show of being tired out, although by this time at night – I mean, by ten o'clock – he would be tired out. But what he was actually saying was that it was past my bedtime too, because Leo always looked after me like a parent, when my parents weren't around.

9

'Oh,' Adam said to me, 'must you go, already? It's only – so early.'

'You go, Leo.' I smiled. 'You go. Adam and I would like to have a walk along the river together, wouldn't we, Adam?'

He nodded, smiling.

'Adam . . .' Leo leaned forward to speak, looking quite serious, especially for him. He made me feel slightly worried about what he was going to say. He seemed to be inspecting Adam, looking for, I don't know – his intentions, something serious like that. 'Adam,' he said, studying the edges of the young Frenchman's handsome face, 'can I ask you, your hair – how do you get such a sheen? It's absolutely – it's beautiful, isn't it, Amy?'

I nodded now, smiling, I think, like a fool. Adam's hair was so dark, so long and shiny that Leo and I could very nearly see our forward-thrusting faces in it. When Adam looked at me, turning his face in my direction, I really could see myself reflected in the dense darkness of his eyes. They were so deep brown, so close to being black, it was practically impossible to distinguish between the pupil and the iris, especially set against the strangely blue paleness of the whites of his eyes.

'Oh,' Adam said, turning from me back to Leo, 'good hair products. French, you see?'

'I see,' said Leo, because he could see, examining Adam's head as if inspecting every strand of hair.

'Before you leave tomorrow,' Adam said, 'I'll bring you some. The same as I have.'

'We'll be leaving very early,' Leo said, but hopefully.

'I'll be there,' Adam insisted. 'Amy and I walk by the Seine for only a small while. I'll see you in the morning,' he said.

Leo took another long look at Adam's hair. Leo's curly brown locks could never achieve such sheen, we all knew;

but Leo looked with such envious longing, he couldn't help but be tempted. 'So be it,' he said, getting up. 'Amy, you must be back and ready to go to bed in an hour. Agreed?'

'Agreed,' I said.

Leo sighed theatrically. 'A few hair products! How cheaply can Lovely Leo be bought off? Sweethearts, tomorrow's another day. Never forget that. It's all change in the morning, right?'

We nodded. Neither of us understood what he was talking about. It didn't matter. Leo said things, whatever came into his head. Most of it didn't mean anything at all. Some of it, though, every now and then something that Leo said would come back to thump you between the eyes with its cleverness, its wiseness or brilliance.

'Oh, he's lovely,' I said, as we walked, looking at the lights from the bridges shining on the surface of the River Seine that runs through Paris, just as the Thames does through London. Paris isn't like London, though. Sometimes it may look similar, but it has a different feel to it. Or at least, it did when I was walking along the embankment with Adam. Paris felt like – like Adam!

'He is part of your team – your management, isn't he?' Adam said. He turned. 'Oh, look,' he said, 'the bird, flying at night. What do you call this bird?'

'A seagull,' I said.

'*Oui*. Yes, seagull. See how it flies above the lights? I love this. So silent.'

Another gull glided over the river, its underside illuminated by the lamps on one of the bridges. 'It's like a ghost,' I said.

11

'Yes,' he agreed, immediately, 'like a ghost. But not afraid, no?'

'No,' I smiled.

We watched the gulls.

'So beautiful,' he said. 'So beautiful.'

'And not afraid,' I said.

One of the gulls cried, with such an eerie, ugly caw. Adam looked at me with his deep, dark eyes. Both made me feel at least wary, if not afraid. The memory of the way Jag Mistri – the dancer I once thought I'd fallen in love with, who had betrayed and hurt me – stirred. What Jag did to me, allowing Ray Ray and Solar Records to control and manipulate my emotions like that, had left behind a little pip of fearful feeling in the pit of my stomach that I didn't want Adam, or anybody else to germinate and grow any bigger.

'No,' I said, 'yes.' I was trying to bring the conversation back round to Leo, but found no, followed by yes, wasn't quite what I wanted to say. 'I mean,' I said, 'getting back to Leo, that he is part of the team. But he's more than that. He's a friend.'

'Oh,' Adam said, smiling, 'you must be covered with friends – friends are everywhere for you, I'm sure. Yes?'

'No,' I said, without following it with another 'yes'. 'No' because I wasn't foolish or blind enough to believe that all the seemingly kind and caring people I met through the music business were friends. The Biz wasn't like that. Everybody was so outgoingly friendly, but most of them, I knew, would do a deal that would stitch everybody else up, and do it gladly and with pleasure.

Knowing this was part of why Adam kept making me feel not quite right about being with him, letting him look at me with those eyes, from that face, framed by that hair. The pop world was like this, presenting a beautiful face while the fists in the pockets were curled around coins.

So, 'No,' I said. 'Not real friends. I honestly think I have very few real friends.'

'But Leo is one of them?'

'Yes. He is. I love him.'

'Love?'

'Yes. Leo's – lovely. He's been hurt, in the past. He looks after me, but I look after him too. We care about each other.'

'Yes,' Adam said, as we strolled on, 'that is a friend. You care about each other.'

'And,' I said, 'there's my best friend, Beccs. Rebecca. She knows me.'

'That's – nice.'

'Yes. I tell her everything.'

'Everything?'

'Yes. My secrets are safe with Beccs,' I said. I knew now, more than ever, that they were. Beccs had inadvertently given me away to the nastier papers through her ex-boyfriend James, telling him about me because she trusted him and he and I were special to her. We'd both learned some hard lessons, Beccs and I; but the important thing was our friendship, that it should remain intact or even strengthened by the horrible things that happened to us.

'Oh, yes,' I said again.

Adam watched me smiling as I thought about Beccs. The look on his face seemed to understand and approve of my feelings for her, giving him the highly dangerous appearance of being sensitive and sincere. I'd need to get to know him a whole lot better if I was ever going to let him get anywhere near being close to me.

Whether I wanted to or not was another question. He, and

13

Paris, made me feel, you know what it's like, when a person and a place, a time or a tune makes you feel wonderful, as if you're the centre of the universe with other people's thoughts and feelings all revolving around you. That walk by the river through Paris with Adam on a still, warm, early September evening was doing everything possible to move me, to turn my heart. Or rather the pit of my stomach; as that always seemed to be where I felt flutterings of fear when afraid, excitement when excited. Adam and Paris were making me feel both in turn, at the same time, attempting to confuse me with conflicting emotions.

'You are lucky,' Adam said. 'I have no friends so close. Pierre, I suppose.'

'Your manager?'

'Yes. Ah, he is also my friend. I trust him. He is a good man. Caring, you understand?'

I laughed, but bitterly. 'I think I understand,' I said. 'But all I can do is compare what you've just said to my manager.'

'Mr Raymond?'

'Mr Raymond Raymond, yes. I tell you, he's nothing like a friend.'

'No?'

'No.'

'Then how can you work together?'

'Good question. The answer is we don't. We don't work together. Ray uses people. He'll use you, and Pierre, if he gets half a chance. Leo – it's a funny situation. Leo loves Ray –'

'He loves him?'

'And he hates him. Leo tries to look after me, but tries to do what's best for Ray, too. He has a hard time of it. Leo's my friend in Solar Records, not Ray. Definitely not Ray.'

'Not Ben?' Adam said.

Ben worked for Solar Records. He was my friend from

school. Adam was obviously trying to put it all together in his head. Ben had been behaving aggressively towards Adam, not really because of Adam, but more to do with what had happened in Ben's past – the joy riding, in particular, that had caused the death of our other friend, dear sweet Geoffrey Fryer. Ben's response had been to pretend not to care, trying to act cool, drinking and smoking, but all the while going to pieces inside.

'Ben is a friend,' I said.

'Maybe not so to me?' Adam smiled. He had such a gentle way of enquiring, such a warm interest it never felt like he was prying.

'He was going through a hard time,' I said. 'He has nothing against you.'

'That is good.'

'Yes. In fact, Ben's worst enemy has always been himself, ever since –'

Adam waited while I paused. 'Ever since the car crash?' he asked, eventually.

I sighed. 'You know about that, obviously. Yes, ever since then.'

'He was your – you and he were –'

'No, not really. We were – attracted to one another, for a while. Nothing came of it.'

'And now?'

I laughed. 'Why do you want to know?'

He laughed now. 'I want to know everything. I want to know *you*, Amy Peppercorn. You!'

Adam smiled at some people as they passed, recognising him, showing recognition, passing by without interrupting us. 'So,' Adam said, standing very, very close to me, 'you have no one special – no one you are seeing, at the moment?'

'Do you?' I smiled up at him.

'Me? No. No.'

'Surely,' I said, 'there are lots of girls after you. I know there are.'

'As there are lots of boys for you,' he said.

'How old are you, Adam?' I asked, as the dark stubble on his face always made him appear unshaven and older. Some of this was because he actually was almost always unshaven, but he certainly looked older than I did.

'I'm nineteen,' he said.

'Nineteen? You look – you don't look nineteen.'

Adam smiled. 'I'm twenty, soon. And you are nearly seventeen. I know.'

'How do you know?'

'It is your birthday, almost. It isn't a secret, is it? Your friend told me. Leo told me.'

I laughed now. 'Leo! I might have guessed.'

'It was a secret, then – your birthday?'

'No. It's just – Leo. If you ever need to know anything, just ask Leo.'

'Then that's good,' Adam said. He looked pleased, tucking his hands into the pockets of his leather jacket. 'We are busy people,' he said.

'Yes,' I said, 'I suppose we are.'

'So,' he said, producing a tiny wrapped package from one of his pockets. 'I should make an opportunity, no? This is for you. For your birthday.'

'Oh. For my birthday?'

'Yes. But open it. As if it's your birthday here.'

The lid of the little box inside came open with a deliberate clack. The pendant stone clasped in gold hanging on a chain turned in the dappled lamplight as I lifted it out. It was brilliantly, gaspingly blue.

'Lapis lazuli,' Adam said.

I had never seen a stone so achingly blue. 'Is it real?' I said, not quite able to believe that such a blue stone could occur naturally.

'Real?'

'Yes. I mean, where would you see such a deep blue stone like this?'

'It's special, no?'.

'Yes,' I said, holding it up, 'very special.'

'From the outside, when this stone is found, it looks like a rock. The loveliness, the beauty is all on the inside.'

I looked at him.

'Then,' he said, 'when it is brought out, see – see how beautiful it is?' As he took it from me and placed it round my neck from behind, gently clipping the chain fast, he turned me to face him. 'How beautiful is that?' he said.

'Oh,' I said, 'listen to you. Always talking about things as if they're beautiful.'

'No,' he said, looking at me, 'only about the things that are.'

'Oh, no,' I said. I was thinking, Oh no! Leo had told me once, no, more than once, quite often, that I had to learn how not to give. Jag Mistri had shown me how right Leo was. But – oh, what could I do, in Paris on a dappled walkway by the seagulled silver river, as the Seine slipped by without judging or condemning anyone, with such ardent eyes as Adam's fixed upon my face? A blue lapis lazuli glow seemed to be shining upwards, kept clasped in place by the chain of ornate low streetlamps linking the lights of one darling bridge over the river with the next. I was trying not to fall for it all, the romantic near-perfection of the place, the time, the temperature, warm, in September. I didn't trust myself. I didn't trust Paris, or blue stones with fantastic names like lapis lazuli. And I didn't trust Adam.

'It is what they say is semi-precious. But to me,' he said, reaching forward to touch the stone as it hung at my neck, 'it is very precious. Not semi, very.'

# ✱✱✱ Three

**S**eptember 27th: my birthday!

October 24th: Beccs' birthday!

A Saturday night, halfway between: perfect for a party! Actually, it was supposed to be a record company do, a sun-bright showy celebration of the fact that the Solar star – the seventeen-year-old singing sensation – had a hit album that had stayed at or near the top of the chart for seven or eight weeks now. It was supposed to be a way of showing Ray Ray's superior success over his European counterpart in France, Pierre Piatta. Ray was about to enter into some kind of partnership deal with Pierre; but everyone knew that to be in partnership with Ray was to be in competition with him.

This party was Ray's way of showing the French, and the world, that he was the one calling all the shots. Leo hadn't told me all of this; I just knew by the big-up bluster of the party, the press presence, pop and film celebrity contingent, the sheer weight of popular application to what should have been a simple little acknowledgement of achievement so far. So what I decided to do was to hijack the proceedings by turning it into an event of my own: or rather Beccs' and my own.

Solar was going to pay for our birthday party, I decided.

'Oh yeah!' Beccs had laughed, when I told her about it.

'Between my birthday and yours. How's that for timing?'

'Right where we'd have planned it.'

'So, shall we plan it? It'll be swamped with pop people and the press,' I'd said to Beccs.

'So,' she had said, smiling, 'am I going to worry if famous people and the papers want to come to my birthday party? Come on! Let's do it! Let's show 'em what being seventeen's really all about. Party!' She was dancing round her little bedroom, turning up the volume on her tiny, but very loud CD player until the bass thumped and so did Beccs' mum, up the stairs to rap on the door to get her to turn it down.

So here we were in her room again, some sounds on the CD – nothing of mine playing – getting dressed together and doing our make-up ready for our shared seventeenth birthday party. You may already know, but I always went to Beccs' house to get ready if we were going out together. It was like a part of it: getting dressed, joking, each helping do the other's eyes and face.

I always went to Beccs', because of my little sisters. I loved them, of course, but they were two crazy three-year-olds running rings round my soft dad, tearing in and out of my room whenever I was there, or crashing about outside if I tried to shut them out. No one could keep them away. They were like a couple of mini indoor-whirlwinds, rattling the windows, registering their presence on earthquake Richter scales up and down the stairs.

Beccs and I had to hurry up: we only had about three-and-a-half hours to get ready. Well, we liked to take our time. I'd arranged the whole day off, which was an unusual thing for me, to have a lie-in in the morning and a long hot bath before making my way over to my friend's house. I was supposed to be all relaxed and chilled out. So was she. As soon as she opened the front door for me she blurted: 'You should see what I've got to wear! Come on! Come on! Quick!'

And she ran upstairs ahead of me in her training gear, dragging my bag of clothes behind her. She was already buzzing with excitement and about to burst out laughing or crying or both, which frequently happened when we were feeling like this.

'Hello, Mrs Bradley,' I was calling back behind me as I ran up after Beccs.

'Put it on, put it on,' I said, as soon as Beccs showed me her new dress. 'Wow!' I cried. 'It's fantastic!'

It was, too. Yellow. So bright, so beautifully cut low on one side of the skirt, so short on the other, with a single shoulder strap and a plunging back. Not the sort of thing Beccs would normally wear: more like something of mine, sent to me free by the designers that wanted me to be seen in their stuff. My friend had obviously fallen in love with this dress. I had to keep fingers and everything else crossed as she went to the bathroom to put it on, hoping beyond hope that it would suit her.

But as soon as she came back in, I gave a yelp of approval, then a scream of ecstasy as she span round and round to show me just how she and the dress were suited to one another.

'Beccs!' I cried. 'It's fantastic! I've never seen you looking – you don't look like that, do you?'

'I know!' she practically shrieked back at me, looking at herself in her long mirror. 'I know! I can't stop looking at myself in it.'

Her mum came in at that point with some tea for us. 'What does she look like in that dress? Amy, tell her, will you?'

'She looks fabulous, Mrs Bradley.'

'Oh, not you too! Well, I wouldn't want to walk down the high street with my daughter wearing something like that.'

'Well, it's lucky we won't be walking down the high street,' Beccs said, slanting a look at me. I smiled. 'And I won't be wearing something *like* this,' Beccs said. 'I'll be wearing this!'

Mrs Bradley tutted. 'Hmm! Well, you wouldn't catch me going out in public wearing something like that,' she said, closing the door behind her on her way out.

Beccs and I stood staring at each other. We had to listen to her mum stumping off downstairs. I thought my head was going to burst. We burst out laughing as soon as the door downstairs banged closed. We laughed and laughed and Beccs went spinning round the room like a ballerina debutante, looking beautiful and really quite slim and very, very fit indeed. The colour was just right for her.

'It makes you look shapely,' I said.

'Shapely? You mean plump I suppose, don't you?'

'I mean beautiful,' I said.

She laughed. 'Beautiful! You're beginning to sound just like your Frenchman.'

I'd been telling Beccs how everything Adam liked was turned 'beautiful'. 'I don't think he's my Frenchman,' I said.

'Oh, he is,' she said, 'if you want him to be.'

'I'm not so sure. Not now.'

'Now? Why now?'

'Oh, you know, he's gone off the boil, I suppose.'

'What, he's stopped phoning you, has he?'

'Yes,' I said.

For a couple of weeks, since my trip to Paris, Adam had

called me on my mobile every day, speaking to me or leaving me voice-messages to say how beautiful he thought our evening out together had been; how beautiful I looked against the blue of lapis lazuli, and how beautiful it was to be beautiful. He made me laugh. I'd started thinking about him at odd times, during the day in the middle of a song, first thing in the morning, last thing at night, that sort of thing. It wasn't what I'd wanted, but Adam just kept popping into my mind, even without looking at the sheer blue stone in the mirror, or somebody else mentioning it. Ben Lyons had seen it, saying, 'Who's that from, as if I didn't know?'

'An early birthday present,' I'd said, and left it at that. Ben was all right; he'd settled down now, concentrating on becoming a record producer and songwriter, without beating himself up continually over what had happened to Geoff Fryer. It would never go away, because it could never be undone. Geoff would always be absent from our lives; that was a fact. Even Ben was learning to live with it. He wasn't trying to hurt himself all the time, or try to feel better by attacking someone else. Ben was fine; both Leo and I were relieved, as we'd both suffered from Ben's wild mood swings in the past.

But tonight – the night of our shared birthday party, with me already seventeen and a couple of weeks, and Beccs with just a couple of weeks to go – the past was the past. Right now we were getting ready to celebrate, with our excitement bouncing off each other. 'Don't let's talk about Adam,' I said, not wanting to deflate the mood we were in. 'Let's talk about us. Sorry I haven't had much of a chance to call round. I've been – you know. Solar. Interviews, all that. Same old same old. How about you?'

'Me? Studying, what else? It's nearly all I do. And I've felt a bit – I don't know, out of it.'

'What do you mean?'

'I mean – feeling funny. It's all the studying. I haven't had enough time to train properly.'

'Beccs, are you sure you're all right?'

'Yeah! It's nothing. I feel great now. I don't want to talk about it. I want to talk about – you know what I want to talk about: Adam!'

'I've told you, he stopped calling –'

'But why?'

'Oh, it happens. Think about it. All those French girls after him.'

'Hmm. Why haven't you called him?' Beccs said.

'I have,' I said. 'I tried his record company.'

'What about his mobile?'

'I don't think he has one.'

'What? What is he, some old boy or something? No mobile?'

'Oh, he's –'

'Everyone's got a mobile,' she said.

'My dad hasn't,' I said.

'That's what I said. What, is Adam some old boy or something?'

'Are you calling my dad an old boy?' I smiled. 'You wait till I tell him.'

She laughed. 'You know what I mean. How old *is* he, anyway?'

'I can't remember. About fifty, I suppose.'

She looked at me quizzically. 'What? No, you idiot, not your dad. Adam. How old is Adam?'

'Nineteen,' I said.

'Mmm,' she said, licking her lips.

She made me laugh. 'He'll be twenty soon.'

'Yummy!' she mewed.

'What are you like?'

'Me? I'm like you. Well, I'm not like you, but I know you, Amy. I've seen the way he looks at you, don't forget – and I've seen the way you like it.'

'Rubbish!'

'Not rubbish! Truth! You like it when he looks at you like that, you know you do.'

'I don't. I hate it.'

'Yeah, like you hate chocolate.'

'Yeah,' I said, about to burst out laughing, 'just like I hate chocolate.'

Beccs' mum came up again a little while after that to find out what all the shrieking was about. 'You two are like a couple of cats, when you get together.'

'Meow!' Beccs scratched.

So, yes, the venue for our birthday party was an entire night-club in the West End of London that had been hired for the night for Beccs and me and our guests. Or maybe not; but that was how we were treating it. Beccs had invited lots of our old school friends, practically all of whom I'd lost touch with. I found myself quite nervous about seeing them again, because I felt they were Beccs' friends now, so they might try to make me feel, kind of, as if I'd been snotty towards them, losing touch like that. But they all wanted to be there – they were *dying* to be there, in fact, Beccs told me, as so many pop music people were coming from Solar records and from Pierre Piatta Fantastique. Some few film people had been invited with friends of friends, along with some other hanger-on type celebs: people famous for being famous. The whole thing was being snapped-up by the press, with special passes for some of the celeb mags and one or two of the friendlier daily papers.

'Barry Bone isn't coming, is he?' Beccs said, on the way there in a Solar limo, just the two of us. Our mums and my dad had gone on before in a cab, to enable the birthday girls to make our big entrance together, just the two of us. That was how I liked it: the two of us. I loved being alone with Beccs. She was my refuge from the monsters of the pop world. The Barry Bone she was talking about was that slime-ball of a newspaper reporter who had almost driven a wedge between Beccs and me.

'No he is not!' I declared. 'He is definitely not invited. The reverse, in fact. I got Leo to contact him and make sure he wasn't planning to turn up anyway.'

'Good,' Beccs said.

'Let's not think about him and his nasty little newspaper,' I said. 'This is our night. You and me, Beccs. We're it tonight, together, nothing else, right?'

'Oh, yes?' she said, with that just-about-to-laugh look on her face. 'And what about when a certain French party arrives?'

'He might not,' I said. 'Anyway, even if he does –'

'I'll want to know why,' she said, 'if he doesn't.'

'I've already told you,' I said, 'I think he's gone off the boil – it's all those lovely French girls.'

'He looked pretty hot last time I saw him.'

'Yeah, well, that was then.'

'Yeah. Pretty hot.' And she picked up the perfectly blue stone that was hanging round my neck. 'Happy birthday,' she said, grinning.

'It's like a film première,' Beccs said, as we pulled up outside the club. 'I don't think I can – in front of that lot, in this dress!'

'Beccs, of course you can. Come on. You look great. You'll be in all the magazines. They'll all be queuing up to get your dress and diet tips, believe me. Come on.'

And I opened the door and took the plunge, pulling Beccs' hand behind my back. But my heel got caught on the carpet, so thick in the back of the car, so that I stumbled and fell, pulling Beccs out face first and we ended up staggering tangled on the kerb as the flash lamps flickered and caught us apparently drunk and falling over each other.

'Amy!' a hack I knew cried out. 'Amy, who's your friend? Hey, girl in yellow!'

'Come on,' I said. 'We're twins!' I yelled. 'We're both seventeen!'

But a great dark wall of dinner jackets formed in flanks down either side of our entrance through the crowd. Beccs and I dashed for cover, coming into the reception together to be met by a blast of champagne corks and party popper streamers and cheering people calling happy birthdays to us both. My dad was in the front with a bright-red nose and a garland of flowers round his neck, and a big bottle of champagne flowing out onto the carpet. Our mums were holding back the barrage of pop and personality persons, like a couple of down-to-earth earth-mothers. That wasn't much of a description of my mum, who was much more urban-wise than that; but when she was with Beccs' mum, they teamed up as if they were as close friends and confidantes as their daughters.

I just managed to get a glimpse of Ray Ray abiding in a dark doorway before a committee of school friends, including Ben and Beccs' cousin Kirsty, accompanied by Lovely Leo, came party-crashing out at us all at once until we were a mad posse impassable in the crowded foyer.

The invited press were interposed at intervals amongst the crowd, flish-flashing and fizzing with enthusiasm like more party-poppers and champagne bottles. There were so many schoolfriends I didn't know where to begin. Beccs took hold of my hand and we dashed for entry into the nightclub arena itself, where Solar staff and friends cheered and waved glasses and drinks bottles, while PPF people raised no wine glass nor drinks bottle because, as far as I could see, none of them was there.

But there was no time to wonder what had happened to all the French people I'd expected to see, including that one particular French person, because there were presents and toasts for Beccs and me as we grinned and were kissed and congratulated as if we'd done something remarkable like won a prize for something very skilful and strenuous.

'We're seventeen!' Beccs shouted, kissing and hugging me.

Her cousin Kirsty came up and flounced over everyone as the press photographers fixed cameras on us. 'We're all seventeen!' Kirsty declared, bending down to kiss me, she was that much taller, covering me in her blanket of long blonde hair.

This was the first time I'd seen her in a very long while. She'd been a member of our school band, Car Crime, with Beccs and Ben and Geoff and me. Her kiss hit my face like a stone; her mouth was so screwed up and horribly hard. If there ever was a peck on the cheek this was it, hitting me like the beak of a very tall and languorous bird. That was it then, after all that time. In an instant she was turning from me to Beccs to put her arms round her as if they were the closest cousins in the whole history of cousin-dom. Beccs was shuffled to one side, towards the first flash of a camera, as

Kirsty was attracted to the press of publicity as if she was a starlet already on an early satellite orbit.

But I was laughing as another young star stood before her in the limelight: my so-called arch pop-rival, Courtney Schaeffer, preened and posed there like the image of pop-perfection that Kirsty would have aspired to, given half a chance. Poor Beccs found herself discarded as suddenly as she had been collected by her cousin. Kirsty flew to Courtney, almost dancing by her side as if they were both part of the same act. Kirsty idolised Courtney, but Courtney looked at her as she would have disdained any gatecrasher.

'Courtney!' I saw Kirsty saying, trying to greet her hero like an old friend. Courtney was backing away, looking for help, getting none. Kirsty was wrapping her in kindliness and hair, hugging and trying to kiss her while Beccs turned, laughing, to me.

'Who invited her?' she said. 'Who invited Courtney?'

I shrugged. I laughed. All sorts of unlikely people had been invited. I pointed to a huge man and a tiny woman, both wearing embroidered kaftans, a sort of long hippie gown, and knitted dangly hats. 'Lord Bartholomew,' I said. 'He owns the safari park. Who would have invited him?'

We both laughed. We were holding hands, going about talking to people. We were constantly dragging each other from one side of the dance floor to the other. Nobody was dancing. There was no music. People were talking. Talking, talking, talking. The Biz people liked it like that.

My old school friends were great, all of them. They made it seem as if they'd all been looking forward to seeing me again after all this time. They wanted to know what it was like, being me, and did I know that pop singer and that film actor. I told them how great it was, being me. They seemed to like it that I thought so.

Ben had turned up not dressed entirely in black as usual; this time he had included white. His black suit had a white pinstripe, with black shirt and white tie. He looked like an old Chicago gangster. He looked great. The girls from school remembered him and were on to him on the instant, those that weren't all eyes for better-known faces, like David Docherty, lead singer with the Motes, or Raphael, one of the boys from La Scala, the opera-rock boy band.

'You know everyone!' Beccs said.

'No, I don't,' I laughed. 'I don't know most of these people.'

'But they all know you.'

Leo caught up with us. He gasped. 'Oh, my! Look at you two! Listen to me, my lovelies – always be seventeen, always.'

We laughed, again. We were almost running round and round in circles, we were so hyped-up.

'No, honestly,' he insisted, hugging us, almost holding us down, 'listen to me. Always be like this. Seventeen. You can always be like this. It's up to you. Oh my my, but I think I'm going to cry.'

And he very nearly did. Maybe he would have, had Mrs Bradley not appeared at his elbow complaining all over again about the way we looked in our pencil-strap dresses and very little else.

'Oh,' Leo gushed, 'you must be Rebecca's mother, surely? Rebecca, why did you never tell me how much you take after your mother? No wonder you have such fabulous skin!'

Mrs Bradley was confused, I could see. She was desperately trying not to be flattered, while at the same time flushing with pleasure.

'This is Leo Sanderson, Mrs Bradley.'

'Please, please, please,' Leo exaggerated, 'please let me in on your secret. Why don't we see if we can get something not too unpleasant to drink, then you can tell me how you manage to keep your complexion. It wouldn't be steroids at all, would it? No? Remarkable!' he gasped, turning momentarily to glance at Beccs and me as he led Mrs Bradley harmlessly out of our way.

We screamed with laughter. My mum came over after a while and screamed with us for a bit.

The Static Cats – Angel, Kaylie and Miranda – the vocal group Ben had been looking after at Solar, arrived and were doing the rounds, trying to get their pictures taken as many times as possible, saying hello to me, smiling wildly at everyone. Then they saw Ben and swooped down upon him. Ben had been contending with Courtney Schaeffer and Kirsty McCloud, who, because they were not friends, seemed to have become rivals for Ben's attention.

'Ben's having a good time,' my mum smiled, 'by the looks of it.' Surrounded by Courtney, Kirsty and the three Cats, of course Ben was enjoying himself.

'Happy birthday to you two.' My dad hiccoughed into view, desperately hanging onto his huge magnum of champagne, lost without the twins.

'Tony,' my mum said, 'how much have you had to drink?'

'Me?' he said, as if only just remembering his name was Tony. 'Me? Hardly anything. Why?' Forgetting about the big bottle he was toting, my dad acted offended at the suggestion that he'd had anything to drink at all. 'Anyway,' he went on, dismissively, 'm\ eldest daughter's seventeen with a successful album at the top of the album charts.'

'That's right,' Beccs said. 'It's only right to celebrate, Mr Peppercorn.'

'Tony,' he said, 'call me Tony.'

Beccs smiled. So did I. We both knew she'd never allow

herself to call him that, not after calling him Mr Peppercorn for all these years.

'Mum,' I said, 'where are the French people? Where are the people from Pierre?' I asked my mum this because she, as much as anyone, would be in a position to know. I'd been expecting dozens of artists and their management from PPF and from the other record company.

'Yes,' Beccs said, nudging me, 'what's happened to Adam Bede this evening? Why isn't he here?'

My mum looked quite worriedly at Beccs and me, then at my dad. I was hoping she was looking so serious because of the amount of champagne my dad might have consumed.

Ray Ray was tapping at the mike on one side of the little stage set where the DJs usually did their stuff behind the mixing tables. Ray's amplified tapping banged for everyone's attention before he cleared his throat and smiled, glancing at me, as if to confirm where I was.

'Yes,' he said. That was Ray's way of being positive, starting off with a yes. 'So,' he went on.

Any chatter that was left sprinkled around the outskirts died down as Ray smiled his most sincere and most harmful smile.

'So far so good,' he champed, halting for a few moments, perhaps for a laugh of appreciation, I don't know. None came. He went on, undeterred. 'It's not so long,' he said, 'since I first saw her. Little girl, big voice. Not just that. Not just that. There's something else. We all know this business. What is it, that something else, in this business? Talent? X-factor? Star quality? You know, and I know, you can't pin it down. Except – except when you see it. You don't see it – you feel it, right? Am I right?'

All round us people were nodding, mumbling.

'Soon as I saw her, that little girl, soon as I heard her, I felt it. And was I right? Was I right?'

The nodding and mumbling tumbled into a ripple of applause and approval. Beccs was holding my hand. My mum took the other. My dad beamed.

'I was right!' Ray exclaimed.

That wasn't quite how I remembered it; that it wasn't nearly that clear-cut and inevitable. But Ray was being kind of poetic, I supposed, in his own Solar-powered way.

'Yes! We've come a long way. Not all been easy. No. Course not. But worth it. Every little thing. Why? Because we showed them. We showed them what we could do. A good team. Songwriters, publishers. The crew. Producers. Management,' he said, with an appalling attempt at humility that looked like a fawning bow. Almost everybody laughed, but I could see Ray hadn't been trying to be humorous there. He gnashed his teeth around another smile.

'And,' he said, with a pause, a florid flourish, 'the girl herself. Little Amy Peppercorn!'

The place applauded – all of it, instantaneously, as if it had been waiting, champing at the bit to let go and fly. Ray waited for the noise to die down. It didn't. He held up his arms like the conductor of an orchestra. If he'd have been holding a white baton, he'd have tapped it then, to bring the orchestra, the players, back down.

'A celebration!' he announced. 'A celebration! This is what Solar – this is what Amy and Solar can do. Amy?' he said, indicating that I should join him up there.

I felt Beccs and my mum guiding me forward, releasing me at the last second before I hopped up next to Ray on the teeny tiny stage. We were having to stand close together, side by side with my shoulder touching his arm, so tight was the available space up there. All of a sudden I felt Ray's serpentine arm slither over my shoulders, to lie there as if about to coil about my neck. There was a rustle as I shivered against the scales. There wasn't really, of course, but another shiver of applause, turned away from warmth by the weight and temperature of the arm pressing me to Ray's side.

'This!' Ray pronounced, producing a framed vinyl record that must have been previously hidden behind the record decks. 'Amy Peppercorn – *If Ever!*' he bellowed, holding the frame above his head so that those back as far as the bar could see it. 'Gone platinum!'

There was a huge cheer from one quarter of the club. The framed record – passed to me and raised for applause for a few moments more – grew heavy in my hands. I was looking for Beccs, hoping to get her to come up on the stage with me, to share our birthday celebration again. But she had turned from me by now, talking away to her cousin Kirsty and to some of the others from school.

Ray Ray was looking at me, with my dad by his side. They were smiling. I handed the platinum award back to him. He handed it on to my dad. I was about to make my way past them and back to my birthday party, our birthday party, which was starting to happen to Beccs and the others without me, but Ray wasn't about to let me through that easily.

'People,' he said, catching me by the arm, leading me where I wouldn't want to go, if only it had been left up to me. 'They want to meet you.'

'Who are they?'

'People!' As he led me astray, to where they were waiting for me in the shadow of the bar: record-company people, people like Ray Ray, smiling. But not really smiling.

So the party started properly at last, with the club DJs mixing their sounds, and the floor filled with everybody, not just my dad, but my mum too, dancing to music that, at my request, was not mine and did not belong to Solar Records. I wanted to ask my mum again what had happened to Pierre, and of course to Adam, but she was having a good time and so was Beccs and so was Ben.

Kirsty and Courtney were in fierce confrontation, competitively dancing, fighting each other for the attention of – of just about everyone. Courtney had a massive head start on Kirsty, being as well-known as she was, but Kirsty was doing unexpectedly well with Ben, which did surprise me, and with Raphael from La Scala, and with Beccs.

From wherever Ray had me positioned as he talked about me to his people, I could see Ben and Raphael talking and laughing together, but also competitively, as Kirsty and Courtney were. Kirsty was being deliberately nice to Courtney, while putting her nose out of joint by flirting with Ben and Raphael, taking over their attention whenever she felt like it. Several times she was photographed with Raphael while Ben inadvertently ignored Courtney.

I wanted to go and join Beccs and Ben. I wanted Kirsty and Courtney to see me with my friends, having a good time, simply. Only that. But record executives like Ray took me by the arm like a platinum commodity, looking me up and down, sizing me up for worth.

'What's going on?' I asked Ray. 'Where's Pierre?'

'No need to worry,' Ray smiled, pointing out my mum and dad dancing together. 'Mum's having a good time,' he said. 'Everyone!' he expanded, flinging out an arm to encompass the whole dancing, talking, laughing nightclub.

'It was supposed to be a birthday party,' I said.

'No it wasn't,' he corrected me. 'It's another opportunity,' he said, turning me away from the celebration to the next in line to meet his Solar star.

# **Four**

'**T**here's someone waiting to see you –'

'No, Leo,' I said. I'd only just escaped, on the pretext of having to go to the loo, but making my way instead to join my friends, now I felt so comfortable with them again. 'I don't want to meet anybody else, so they can just –'

'No,' he said, 'Lovely, listen. He's waiting outside.' He glanced over at the bar. 'Don't ask me anything, Sweet. Just go outside. Now.'

'Now?'

'Go,' he said, going from me, skirting the edges of the space he conceived as belonging to Ben, approaching my mum and dad as they stood talking together on the edge of the dance floor. He didn't glance back at me.

I made my way out into the foyer. The place was still quite busy, with late arrivals being checked in at the door, being let in, some turned away. The big guys on the door were stuffed into white dinner jackets. There was a very pretty girl with a list, against which she was checking everybody's name. The big white dinner jackets backed her, debarring or allowing, either way with a look of extreme disapproval on their faces whenever a man was allowed in, complete indifference if it was a woman. But nobody seemed to be actually waiting to see me, although most of them faltered and looked, smiling and wondering whether or not to speak to me.

'Oh,' the girl with the list of names looked back and called to me, 'sorry. There's someone out here. Says he has to see you.'

I went to the front door. Standing to one side, trying not to get in anybody's way, leather jacket, jeans, long dark hair. 'You're here!'

'Yes,' Adam said, smiling, reaching for my hands. He took them, drawing me to the side with him. 'I'm here.'

'Why are you waiting out here?'

'I cannot come in.'

'What?'

'They have this list – I'm not – but you look – are you warm, out here? Warm enough?'

'I don't understand. You can't get in?'

'You're wearing it. Lapis lazuli.'

Oh, you know, the way he said it – lapis lazuli – was as if the blue stone was the most exquisitely expensive mineral in the world. It was what was called 'semi-precious', but not to me. Just the name alone valued it above the gold of the chain that clasped and held it.

He reached forward and lifted the stone from the base of my neck. 'It looks beautiful.'

'But why are you out here?'

'You don't know?'

'No. What's happened?'

'Things – these things happen. Pierre, he wants one thing, Ray wants –'

'Ah!' I said, suddenly falling in. 'Ray wants something else, doesn't he? Ray wants it Ray's way, always. You're going to tell me that Pierre and Ray have fallen out over this –'

'Fallen out?'

'Argued.'

'Not Pierre, you understand.'

'Oh, I understand. I understand all right. Ray has thrown a wobbler –'

Adam looked a question at me.

I smiled. Annoyed as I was, I couldn't help it. With Adam looking questioningly at me like that, with that almost but not quite amused look on his face, what else could I do? 'You're coming in,' I said, offering him my hand.

'I wanted only to wish you happy birthday,' he said, kissing me on one cheek. One cheek, from this gorgeous Frenchman, kissed slowly like that, was far more meaningful and intimate than any two-faced showbiz double-peck. 'Happy birthday,' he said. 'I'm very happy to see you wearing the lapis lazuli on your birthday.'

'I haven't taken it off since you gave it to me,' I said, unexpectedly. I say 'unexpectedly' because for one, I hadn't expected to say it, and two, it wasn't meant to sound as flirtatiously meaningful as it obviously did. More than that, though, was that I wasn't expecting to feel as I did when I said it, as if I meant it to be meaningful, which I hadn't, to begin with. Then, I suppose, I had meant it. My own emotions were taking me unawares. Adam was looking at me. He could see how confused I was, so he simply smiled and let me get away with it.

'I don't want to spoil anything, here,' he said, pointing towards the entrance to the club.

'You won't spoil anything. I thought you were invited, you and Pierre, and the others.'

'I think yes, then no,' he said.

'Well, you're invited now. Come on, let's go in together.' But Adam was reluctant. 'Please, Adam. You're my guest. My special guest. It's my birthday and I'll have who I like at my party.'

'And you like me?'

'Yes,' I said. 'I like you.'

We were looking at each other. The danger of such a look felt like excitement in the pit of my stomach. Still I was too afraid of where it might lead. I wasn't ready, not yet, not so soon after – after everything else that had gone before. I needed to gather my thoughts, to get back in control of my emotions – not get back, because I don't think I'd ever been in any kind of control before. But now I wanted control. It was important to me, and becoming more and more import-ant as I went on. For that reason, I resisted the temptation to kiss Adam outside the club, choosing to wait until I was good and ready, if I ever was.

'So come in with me,' I said, quietly, 'will you?'

He nodded. He didn't try to kiss me. That made me feel more like wanting to kiss him. Too confusing! Too out of control! If I'd learned anything from Ray in the time I'd known him, it was how valuable control was. I didn't want anyone taking advantage of me, ever again.

'Come on then,' I said, taking control, leading my special guest in by the hand. 'He's with me,' I said into the pretty smile of the girl on the door. The door managers shifted the bulk inside their white jackets.

Adam and I went in to my party together, picked out immediately by the press present, snapped on ready camera to be presented soon as a couple, whether we liked it or not. I wasn't sure what I liked.

No, I liked Adam. He danced with me as soon as we could make it to the floor. All the eyes were upon us, most wonder-ing where this handsome young man had sprung from. Some, though, were not wondering. There were eyes that looked knowingly, like my mum's and my dad's. Or strange looks, strange like Ray's, glowering out of the depths of the shadows in the corner by the bar. Kirsty and Courtney eyed one another for a moment, before looking back at me.

I was with Adam and it did feel good. Everyone was looking at us. Everyone except Beccs, for some reason. For a while I couldn't find out where she was – then, when I saw her dancing all on her own, she didn't acknowledge the fact I now had Adam with me. Beccs looked engrossed in what she was doing, oblivious to what was going on around her, but everyone else had seen us together.

Beccs may not have noticed anything, but Adam certainly did. He always noticed everything. 'You are not relaxed,' he leaned forward to say into my ear.

For a moment, as Ray appeared on the edge of the dance floor, I thought he was about to come and drag me away. His face looked all screwed into too small a segment of his head.

Adam pretended not to see him. Leo fussed on through and took Ray away with him. I'd never seen Leo do such a thing. I hadn't even thought such a thing was possible. But Ray went with him, back to the bar scattered with record labels, to the rivals laughing competitively, slapping each other and buying drinks for everyone with such force and malice. That was Ray's world.

Kirsty had abandoned, for the moment, her feud with Courtney, leaving the singer to compete with only the three Static Cats for Ben's concentration, to join her cousin on the dance floor. They touched hands and laughed. Kirsty glanced over at me, at Adam, at me. Beccs looked to see what she was looking at.

With such relief I saw Beccs see me there with Adam for the first time. She genuinely hadn't noticed us, I could tell by her reaction, the way she immediately ran over to say hello to

Adam, to kiss him, to kiss me too. 'You're here!' she shouted over the loudness of the dance music.

'I'm here!' Adam called back to her over the few centimetres of expanse between them. 'I couldn't miss Amy's birthday!'

Beccs said something back. Adam couldn't hear it; neither could I. He leaned his ear closer to her. She said again what she'd said before. I was still too far away to hear.

Adam smiled. 'I didn't know,' he shouted.

'What?' I said. 'What was it?'

'It's Beccs' birthday!' he announced, almost as if he thought I wouldn't have known.

'It's my birthday too!' Beccs shouted out, loud enough for us both to hear: loud enough for lots of people to hear.

But nobody but Adam and I heard it; nobody was listening. Beccs turned to go. All round us, the competitive cacophony: Ray's noisy silence seethed amongst his music-magnate enemy-associates, the cut-throat, self-interested pirates surrounding him, with only Lovely Leo as his accompanist and one sure ally; the Kirsty/Courtney duet continued over Ben, with backing and wailing harmonies by the Static Cats; my old-school chorus trilled like larks ascending. Everyone was dancing all round me, but all I saw was my best friend walking away from me on our birthday.

I went after her, leaving Adam there on his own, touching her shoulder, turning her. She looked at me. 'Come back,' I said into her ear. 'Come back and dance with us.'

She looked over my shoulder at Adam. She shook her head, before hugging me. 'No,' she said, 'you go. Go on. He's waiting for you.'

'Are you all right?' I said. We were holding each other. 'I'd rather stay with you.'

'No,' she said. 'I'm all right. Really.'

And we looked at each other. We were all right. We were fine. Beccs nodded. She laughed. One of my songs had started to play: *Love Makes Me Sick*.

Something made me feel as if tears could come. 'You're my best friend,' I said into my best friend's ear.

'And you're mine,' she shouted back. 'Now you'd better go and do something about Adam,' she said, hugging me again, looking over my shoulder, 'before somebody else does.'

She laughed and turned me round to show me where the Cats had deserted Ben for the moment and had homed in on Adam, obviously working their way round to him from all sides without apparently noticing him in the direct flight-path of their dance trajectories.

I laughed too, especially as Beccs slid me forward towards him with a push of approval from behind, intercepting the others' attack, positioning myself in front of advancing Miranda like one of Beccs' football defenders. Glancing back at Beccs, I pretended to fall against Adam. She gestured like a goal-scorer. I gestured back.

Adam laughed. '*Bon anniversaire!*' he sang out. 'Happy birthday!'

'Can I tell you something?' Adam was saying, as we sat at one of the tables along the platform in front of the bar, over-looking the dance floor.

'You can tell me something,' I said, taking a break from a long, long drink of refreshingly cold orange juice. 'Of course you can tell me something,' I joked, 'but only if you think I'm really going to want to hear it. Is it about the Static Cats? Do you like them?'

It was so nice to see his smile as he sat opposite me. My

hands were on the table. So were Adam's. He looked as if he were about to reach for me, although he seemed to be resisting the urge.

'Miranda's very – straightforward,' he said.

'Straightforward?' I said. 'Yes, I suppose you could call it that.'

At the bar behind us, a raucous roar of male laughter. My dad was in amongst it somewhere, with Ray Ray. So was Leo, but this noise was nothing to do with his kind of self-deprecating giggle. This was massive with male pride and aggression. A particularly ugly sound; the buzz of bar-flies amongst the proper birthday-party goers.

'But you,' Adam was saying, 'you are always thinking so much. Always you are looking around and thinking things.'

'Am I?'

'Always. Looking around, listening, looking, listening, thinking. Thinking, thinking, thinking.'

I laughed as he was speaking. 'Okay, okay. I get the picture.'

'Do you? Yes, I think you do. You are always getting pictures, no?'

'How do you mean?'

'Always pictures, impressions. Always you are so worried about – about this, about that.'

The way he was flinging his arms about made me laugh again.

'Oh,' he said, trying to be serious. 'Oh, you do know things. You know a great many things.'

'Do I? Like what?'

'Like – let's say, you know how much you worry, worrying about all things and everything. All about you, you look, you listen, you care. Why do you do this?'

'I just want –'

'No. I mean something other – else. I mean, why worry, and not do something?'

'Like what?'

'Anything. Whatever worries you, do something for it. To stop it. If something worries you, then do something to . . .'

He tailed off, because I was obviously trying hard not to laugh. 'So that's what you do, is it?'

'Yes,' he said, seriously.

I liked his seriousness so much. It looked a lot like honesty, I supposed. I believed him. 'But there's always so much I can't do anything about,' I said. 'This business, the press, you know.'

'No,' he said, 'I don't. It doesn't need to be like that. It doesn't. No – honestly.'

Honestly, he said, as if I might not have believed him. Although I didn't see how he could have so much more control than me, he convinced me anyway. I wanted to believe him. 'I suppose because you write your own songs,' I said, 'things are different for you.'

'Yes. No. It is that, but not because of that. Pierre insists I write my songs. I write with other people, better musicians. They are good.'

'But you're involved,' I said.

'Yes,' he said, 'and so could you be. You could be more involved in what happens to you.'

'You think so?' I asked. He was nodding. I wanted to believe him, but as he finally reached out across the table to take my hand, the laughter from the bar roared at us, disapproving laughter, with no fun in it, entirely and irrevocably out of my control.

When Adam had to go, that was when he kissed me. He'd done it before, on stage and so on, but this – this was different, very different! We were – well, we were out of harm's way, in a recess where we could be alone for a minute or two. 'I won't let you go,' he whispered, holding me.

'You'll have to,' I said. 'You have to go.'

'No,' he said, softly.

He kissed me then. I wanted him to and he did. It was a special night. I hadn't envisaged spending so much time with Adam; but I couldn't separate myself from him. He was there. He was serious. There definitely was something special about his seriousness, as if I could learn from him. No, not learn: as if he was good for me. He certainly made me feel good. I think I'd started to trust him. It didn't seem at all as if he wanted to hurt me, to use or manipulate me.

Anyway, he had to go. On my way back in, I saw Beccs' mum asleep on one of the sofas in the chill-out section. Beccs was doing all right. I don't think she'd left the dance floor all night. Neither had my mum, much. She had so much energy. It was great! The three of us danced together, laughing, like three girls out on the town. The Cats came along and joined us, six girls out then, having a wonderful time.

'Where's Adam gone?' Miranda asked, looking about. She didn't look like she was really expecting an answer, so I didn't answer.

I don't know what had happened to my dad or to Ray Ray. Leo reappeared though, dancing with the girls, showing us all how to do it.

'Be careful!' Leo leaned in close to my ear to say.

I nodded. 'Yes!' I shouted. 'Don't worry!'

Leo loved me, and I loved him, but sometimes I think we bounced worries off each other too much. Like this, having this much fun, I really didn't know why we did it all the time. I really didn't have a clue why we bothered.

It was just a great night.

# ⁎⁎⁎ Five

It was a great night!

Not until about three o'clock in the afternoon did I get to Solar the following day. After a night like that, my brain wouldn't switch off. It kept going over and over everything that had happened. Adam seemed to be with me, all night, being serious, telling me again and again to take more control, take more control.

'Yeah,' Ray said, having sent for me, summoning me into the platinum-disc-adorned walls of his office, 'but it's over now.' He had a yo-yo amongst the other trinkets and junk on his desk.

'Great night, though,' I said, fitting the yo-yo string onto my finger.

Ray watched me yo, then yo. 'No,' he said, watching me steadily as my yo-yo went twistingly wrong, tangling in its own string, and was left dangling. 'I mean all that with Pierre. With PPF.'

I felt apprehensive. 'But what about –' I said, faltering, replacing the tangled yo-yo, 'what about the European release for the singles, the album? What about the –'

'Leave it!' he said, picking up the yo-yo, tugging at the string. 'It'll be sorted.'

'Yes, but –'

'That's it!' he said, now everything was wound up again,

just as he liked it. He pulled the string tight. Ray always pulled too hard on the strings.

'But, what about –'

He stopped me: not by saying anything, but by breathing in. Ray's sharp inhalation was like the warning of danger from a snake. 'That's all,' he said.

His attitude confused me, as it was designed to. That's what he did, confusing and intimidating, frightening people. His every explanation felt like a threat. Ray's final statement was as always exactly that: final.

But still I faltered. He'd actually dismissed me, his thinking forehead already creasing into the future. I wasn't supposed to have anything to say about it. 'It's the wrong decision,' I went and said, before I could stop myself. The confusion had suddenly cleared from my mind: Ray was dismissing me and ending his collaboration with Pierre.

'It's the wrong decision,' I said, suddenly understanding, reacting too quickly.

Everything stopped. Ray's forehead cleared of forward-thinking as he slowly sat back, inhaling with serpentine deliberation, a slight smile appearing at the corners of his scaly mouth. For a long, long time, neither of us spoke. Everything, all we might yet say, every possibility seemed to hang in the air between us.

'So,' he said, at long last, 'seventeen, now, isn't it? Happy birthday, was it?'

'Yes,' I said, as if defending myself for being seventeen.

'Good party,' Ray said, making a statement.

I nodded.

'Let's keep it a good party.'

'I don't know what you're talking about.'

'Don't spoil it, girl. I said, that's it.' He was glaring at me. 'Now go!'

No, I wanted to try to say. But what then? What did I have with which to argue against him?

My single, *Love Makes Me Sick*, had been doing pretty well in the charts. Leo and I were rehearsing it again in preparation for a TV appearance on the *Chart Toppas* show.

'I don't know what's going on,' Leo said. 'I'm as in the dark as you.'

'No you're not, Leo. Talk to me.'

'Sweet, what do you want me to say? Yes, so many arrangements were being made with Pierre. Europe, America. It'll all still happen.'

'Will it? Who says? You? Ray?'

'Be careful, Lovely.'

'Leo, you're always saying that to me. Why should I always have to be careful of everything? Why is everything always set to do me harm if I'm not careful?'

'Oh, my, my! Sweet, come here.'

'No, Leo. Leave me alone!'

He stepped back. He looked at me with a pained expression. 'Listen,' he said, 'girl talk, yes? Home truth time. Okay?'

I nodded.

He glanced about, theatrically. Leo liked to exaggerate his actions, playing the pantomime Dame to make me laugh.

I had to laugh. 'Leo, you are such a –'

'I know,' he exaggerated, flipping his hands. 'I know, don't bother telling me. Just listen, right? Right? Ray.'

That's all he said. I waited for him to go on. But he looked about again.

'Is that it?' I had to say, at length.

'Not enough said? Lovely, listen to me. Last night. Adam. You understand?'

I sighed. 'Leo, you're beginning to sound like Ray. Please try to put complete sentences together, would you? What are you trying to tell me?'

But Leo looked, glancing pantomime left and right before looking straight at me. He pulled a face and shrugged his shoulders.

'You're telling me,' I told Leo, 'that Pierre and Adam, or anybody from PPF, were not wanted, and Adam shouldn't have been there. That's what you're telling me, isn't it? No, that's not a question. Ray didn't want Adam there, did he? He wanted to make it something else, something to do with him and Solar and my – no, *his* career, his business, but I wasn't letting him, was I? No question, Leo. Don't bother answering. I know all this. We both know.'

Leo nodded.

'What we don't know,' I said, 'or at least what I don't know, is how much control Ray thinks he has over what I do – I mean everything I do.'

Leo's head moved so that he was looking at me out of the corner of his eyes. His look said everything.

'Everything,' I said, because his look said that. 'He thinks – even with my friends, with Adam, Ray thinks he can – he thinks he can –'

Leo's expression was one of pity.

The last thing I wanted was pity. 'He can't do that, Leo. I'm not having it! You can tell him if you like, please do!'

He shook his head.

Just then, through the round, soundproofed windows of the studio, I saw Ben arriving with the Static Cats. They saw me looking over at them and waved. I waved them in, passing Leo to open the door to them. 'Hey!' I cried.

51

'Hey!' Ben called back.

'Great party!' the girls said.

'Yeah, great party.'

'Thanks,' I said. 'But listen. Do you remember the time we all did *Love Makes Me Sick* in here?' I said, remembering just that.

The Cats were nodding, smiling. Ben was approaching with a look of curiosity on his face.

'You were really good,' I said. 'Weren't they, Ben? That day we did that song, before you-know-who came along and spoiled it.'

'They were good,' Ben smiled. 'They are good. If they don't make it, there's no justice in this world.'

'There's justice in this world,' I said.

Leo was shaking his head as if there wasn't.

'There is justice in this world,' I said again.

# ✦✶✦ Six

**D**id you see it – that *Toppas* show with the three Cats and me? Leo did a new arrangement of *Love Makes Me*, and he and Ben rehearsed us for the show. The Cats were – well, if you saw it you won't need me to tell you how good they were. They just *were*. Not like backing singers, nothing like that. It was the Cats and me, not me backed by a cat-chorus. It was their first ever TV appearance, although you'd never have known it. I was more nervous beforehand than they were. I spent almost the whole hour before going on psyching myself up, which actually means trying not to feel sick, while they laughed and joked in the room next to mine, running about and banging doors like three young girls on a sleepover at midnight. That was about the first time I came to realise what it was with me – why I was always, as Adam had said, looking about, listening, concerning myself with every single little thing; I was always on my own in times like these.

So I left my room and went to theirs with them. For a few moments, when I first appeared, the Cats stopped and looked at me, wondering if they were about to be told off. Can you imagine: I was like some figure of authority to them? So all I did was laugh, and so did they and soon the four of us were running wild and I'd stopped thinking about things and everything and started to relax. Just before a show, and there I was, having fun, having a laugh, messing about, enjoying myself.

Leo appeared, with a look on his face like everybody's mum, and gave us all a telling off, good and proper. 'What on earth do you think you're doing?'

We were all trying desperately not to laugh.

'You have got a performance to prepare for, you know. Ten minutes, that's all you have. You'd better just be ready, that's all!'

But the dressing room was one big scream. We were all over the place. Not one of us was anywhere near ready.

Ready or not, we went on. Did you see it? That bit where we all broke down into fits of laughter, right in the middle of the song – wasn't that something? Then we were each shoving the other out of the way to be in front of the television camera. We were not singer and backing singers, but four girls doing the song together, or not, as we jostled each other out of the camera lens.

We were laughing the whole way through:

*Falling down all over the place*
*Laughing like a lunatic*
*A look of madness on my face*
*Something's making me feel sick.*

From up there on the stage I could see Ben smiling and Leo fussing, but I could also see how much the audience laughed and sang with us and enjoyed what we were doing almost as much as we did. We pulled it together close to the end of the song and delivered it something like as we'd done during our rehearsals back at Solar.

*But I'd rather feel*
*So very ill*
*Than never be in love at all.*
*Yes, I'd rather feel*
*So very ill*
*Than never be in love at all.*

*Love makes me sick*
*But I can't take a pill*
*Love makes me sick*
*I must like being ill*
*Love makes me sick*
*And gives me such a thrill.*

As we went from the stage with our arms round each other, one of the Cats, Angel, turned to me and said, 'It must be really great being you.'

I laughed. She'd said exactly what that other girl had said to me in Leicester Square.

'No,' I laughed again, 'it's not always this great. I'd rather be a Static Cat,' I said.

Angel laughed now and hugged me as if she was grateful that I'd said such a thing, as if I'd said it out of kindness. But I believed what I was saying. Being Angel or Kaylie or Miranda would always mean being a Cat, part of something, something possibly three times as strong as being just Amy Peppercorn; or possibly infinitely stronger than that. Angel didn't know how serious I was. But I meant it; I'd much rather have been a Static Cat.

# ✳✳✳ Seven

'**I** didn't sanction that,' Ray said. Then he pushed his door to, closing it on me, as I'd been standing in the corridor just outside his office. He didn't slam the door in my face. In so many ways, I wished he had. Ray's wild-man mad temper was so much easier to take than this deliberate freeze.

I shivered. Ray must have been waiting for me to arrive at Solar, sending for me as soon as I'd appeared downstairs.

Coming back down now, still trying to warm up, I turned the corner and into one of the main studios. Nothing was happening. Nothing. That never happened, nothing happening during the day. There was always something going on. All the sound technicians and session musicians were gathered at one end. They looked up at me. Nobody said anything. Then they all broke up, bustling away from their huddle, bursting out like busy ants, each with something suddenly pressing to do.

'What's happened?' I said to one of the technicians. 'What's going on?'

He shook his head.

Big Ron, the studio manager, with a huge pair of earphones on, was fiddling over one of the sound consoles. There was nobody in any of the sound booths, nobody playing or singing in the studios. Ron wouldn't have been mixing any pre-recorded stuff either, because I knew Ron didn't do that. All Ron was doing was lying low, like everybody else, pretending to be busy, looking the other way as I approached, left or right of me, above or below.

I went right up to him. 'Ron! What's going on? What's happening?'

Ron reluctantly took off the protective earphones. 'You seen Ray?' he asked.

I nodded, thinking, Oh no! 'What's he done?' I said.

'He's laying people off,' Ron said. He shrugged. 'Happens all the time in this business.'

'Sacking people?'

'Nah, not really. The music business is like that. They come, they go.'

'Who?'

'Whoever. Some of the session boys. The techs. Producers. Acts.'

'Who? Specifically.'

'Alex, the sound man.'

'Alex?'

Ron nodded.

'Who else, Ron?'

Ron blinked, twice. 'Don't ask me,' he said. 'Ask Ray. Just ask Ray.'

I couldn't. Ray was too white-hot, too nuclear. He had grey lips and a strangely pale face. Even speaking to Ray, about anything, would have been counter-productive or harmful at that moment. Leo would know what had happened, but he wasn't there. He should have been, but he wasn't. I called him, trying, but failing to keep the frustration from my voice. 'Where are you?'

'Oh,' he said, as my voice exploded over the mobile line.

'Good morning to you too, my sweet. How lovely to hear from you.'

'Leo,' I said, still attempting to tone down the urgency, 'something's going on. Where are you?'

'I'm at home, Lovely. I'm working here today.'

'Leo, you never work at home. What are you doing there?'

He was silent. Then, 'I'm keeping out of harm's way,' he admitted. 'I've been thoroughly reprimanded. So have you, by the sound of you. We shouldn't have done it, sweet.'

'Done what?'

'That stuff with the Cats. With Ben. We've stepped out of line again, Lovely. And I'm not – I don't think I can – Ray's mad.'

'I know he is! Don't tell me now!'

'No, I – I'm sorry, I should have warned you. I should have warned Ben. He could have warned them.'

'Warned them? Who?

'Hasn't anybody told you?'

'No. Ron told me some of the studio people have gone – oh no! Who else? Tell me who else!'

'I am, sweet, I am. It's those girls. It's the Cats.'

'No!'

'Lovely, listen –'

'No!'

'Lovely, whatever you do, don't –'

'No!' I shouted again.

'Amy, don't you –'

'No!'

Then another 'No!' but to nobody; nobody but myself as I ran back upstairs to the Solar offices, along the corridor to Ray's angry room. It was tightly shut against me, threateningly closed. On the other side I knew it was big, but still somehow claustrophobic, like Ray himself, showing me space, room to breathe and move, while he held me in one place and constricted me, squeezing me tighter every time I exhaled until I couldn't breathe in without his generosity and kind permission.

## ★**⁺★Eight**

**M**y dad tried to rant Ray-wise, but lacked Ray's power or madness or the will to do anybody any harm. My little sisters Jo and Georgie controlled and manipulated him, when he was supposed to be responsible for them, showing him up for the softie he was. 'It's the business!' he tried to roar, as Ray had. 'You're in the music business – it's tough, that's all there is to it.'

But Jo and George were pulling his ears as he said it, a twin bouncing on either side of him. Neither they nor I were threatened by his pleading insistence. 'You do what you have to do. That's all there is to it.'

'Shut up, Tony,' my mum said.

He did.

I wished I could have said the same to Ray earlier that day. If only 'Shut up, Ray' would do it occasionally, I wouldn't have had to be pinned back against his office wall by the very ferocity of his rage.

'What makes you think!' he'd bellowed at me. 'What makes you! It's nothing to do with what you think! Your little thoughts are nothing! Nothing! And you tell me! You dare tell me!'

With a dreadful swipe of his forepaw, Ray had swept half his cluttered desk clean of the bric-a-brac, the yo-yos and photos, the big dice, token stones, pens, pencils and sharpeners, the fossils and frogs, sending them leaping and flying into wood of chair and metal of filing cabinet with a crash and a fall and a smash of two huge fists down onto naked desktop.

'You! Who are you to tell me!'

'What did you say to him?' my mum was saying, bringing me back to the present, our little living room, the twins bouncing like broken bric-a-brac, my flushed foolish dad, my worried mum, and me. 'What did you say to him, exactly?' she said, warning my dad, with a single glimpse, to keep out of it.

'I told him I didn't like what he'd done.'

My dad shook his head. Both my mum and I knew he'd have been given the Ray Ray version, that he'd have been primed with Ray's reasons and single-sided opinions.

'Shut up, Tony,' my mum said, before he could say anything.

His mouth dropped open. One of the twins, with lightning reflexes, dropped a stray plastic brick into it, where it sat on his tongue like an everlasting red sweet.

'Exactly,' my mum said to me. 'Tell me exactly what happened.'

So I said how it was when I'd got to the studios, with everyone either sacked or shell-shocked, and how I'd marched up to Ray's office to confront him. I had to admit how I'd lost it and surprised us both by accusing him of taking his silly little frustrations out on other people, just because I'd done something with Ben and the Static Cats he didn't approve of. I'd told him, I had to admit, that I thought he was a monster and a control freak and a megalomaniac, since Leo had taken the trouble to teach me the word. Once I'd started I couldn't stop myself. It all came tumbling out, exactly what I thought of him, of how despicable it was that he had to control everyone and everything in the harmful way he did, using people, abusing and discarding them as if he – as if he was God or something!

My dad's head was going from side to side. He was letting the twins take it in turns to remove the red brick and put it back in again.

But my mum looked even more worried. If she'd have shaken her head or tutted or even blinked it would have been far preferable to the shock of the stare she had fixed into my eyes. My dad's disapproval was expected, and always came to next to nothing; my mum's stare interrogated me as if some kind of torture was about to follow. 'Go on,' she said, instinctively knowing there was more.

'I told him,' I said, swallowing, 'that he was stupid to reject the French like that and if he thought he could stop me seeing Adam he had another thing coming.'

The twins laughed. They were having such fun.

'Go on,' my mum said again.

I swallowed again. 'I told him I wanted more control over what I – over everything. I said I was sick of being pushed around and ordered here and there, and I was sick of seeing everyone else used and abused by him. I said – I told him I wanted to start doing things my way.'

My mum kept staring, staring.

'Or,' I said, 'I said I wouldn't be doing things any more.'

'You can't –' my dad tried to say, as one of the twins had just unbricked his mouth.

'Tony!' my mum said.

It was enough to brick him up again.

For a while I thought my mum was going to react along with my dad, along with Ray, against me. I should have known better.

'So,' she said, coolly, 'what did he have to say about that little lot?'

'Not much,' I said. Which was the truth. Ray never said much about anything, just a few unfinished or disjointed sentences.

'Who are you!'

'Who are you to!'

'Speak to me!'

'Not much,' I said.

My dad let out a kind of humphing sound. 'That took self control,' he said, almost under his breath.

We glanced at him.

'He swiped everything off the top of his desk. He smashed his fists down, he broke a big ashtray. He punched the door.'

I had thought, for one terrifying moment, that he was going to punch me; but didn't bother mentioning that fact.

'If that's what you call self control,' I said, directing this at my dad but still looking at my mum, 'then I'd hate to see what out of control looks like.'

My mum and I exchanged long, long looks, while the twins tossed an assortment of soft toys from the back of the settee, plop and plop and plop, over my dad's head and onto the floor in front.

'And,' she said, my serious mum, 'what should you have done?'

The soft toys plopped and plopped then stopped.

What should I have done?

The twins flew over the back of the settee, bounced once one either side of my watching waiting father before landing on the floor ready to throw all the toys back where they came from.

'Why didn't you come and speak to me?' my mum said.

That's what I should have done. But I didn't even do it now; I just looked at her.

'Isn't that my job?' she asked. 'Or have I got it wrong? Isn't that what I'm supposed to do?'

As I looked into my mum's face, I could hear my dad, breathing.

'Shut up, Tony,' she said, still looking at me.

'Me?' he said, affronted. 'What have I said?'

'Nothing,' she said, glancing at him, 'but we could hear what you were thinking, couldn't we, Amy?'

I had to let out a laugh. 'I lost my temper,' I said.

'Yes,' she said, going over to ruffle my dad's hair, or what little of it was left on top. 'You lost your temper.'

The girls, given a good example, both set about ruffling the top of my dad's head, as if to buff away that last remaining tuft. 'You little monkeys!' he cried, flipping them onto their backs on the settee, flicking their bare kicking feet.

'You both lost your tempers,' my mum said, above the uproar of my sisters' screams and my dad's playful growls. 'Both you and Ray.'

'He frightened me,' I said, so that my dad wouldn't hear. 'He really frightened me.'

'I'll see to it,' she said.

'See to what, Mum? What about the Static Cats? What about them?'

'Just wait a while,' she said. 'Just hold on for a bit. I'll get busy.'

I called Angel Iago, the Static Cat. She and I had been getting on quite well. I felt bad for her. And for the other two, of course: they were all Cats together, which was still something, but I'd noticed Angel was more on her own than Kaylie and Miranda, who always seemed to hang out together. 'It's not your fault,' she said, although I couldn't help but think how she and the others must have been thinking it was. I told her about my mum.

'I'm not sure the others want to stay with Solar, anyway,' Angel said. 'Not after the way we've been treated.'

'Only by Ray,' I said.

'Ray *is* Solar,' she said, 'isn't he?'

What could I say?

Beccs and I had a very brief chat that night, but she was studying hard now, starting on the final year of her A-Levels as she was. I had an idea of just how much study-time she'd wasted last term on James Benton and all the trouble and ill-feeling that came with him.

'It's Angel and the other Cats I feel sorry for,' I said.

'It's not your fault,' she said. She sounded almost half-hearted, as if she was just running through the motions.

'Beccs,' I said, 'are you all right?'

'Yes,' she said. 'I've got a headache, that's all.'

'You sure?'

She laughed. 'Of course I'm sure. I'm studying too hard. I lost too much time last term, what with James, and everything. My English and Science really suffered.'

'I know how you feel,' I said, having messed up my Maths studies so badly at school myself.

Another brief silence passed us by.

'Hey!' she said, snapping the silence. 'Guess what? I've decided what I'm going to study at uni next year.'

'Have you? What is it? Sports science?'

'No.'

'Sports psychology?'

'No.'

'No? What then?'

'Law!'

'Law?' I laughed. 'Beccs, you're really something. Law? I never even knew you were interested?'

'Yeah,' she said, 'I want to go to Cambridge, if I can.'

'Cambridge! Beccs!'

'I've been thinking about it for a long time. Without telling anyone,' she added. 'You're the only one I've told, other than my mum.'

'And what did she say?'

'She's dead pleased. She thinks I'm going to be a top barrister and make loads of money.'

'Well, why not?'

'I want to do something good. Law can give me so many opportunities. I want to make a difference.'

'So do I,' I said.

And so I did. Just being lucky, which was all I'd been so far, wasn't enough. I wanted to make a difference, to make things happen. Some time ago, on a TV chat show, I'd said there are two types of people: those that make things happen, and those that let things happen to them. I'd been hoping I was the first type, but I wasn't. Beccs was. Ray Ray was. Adam was, or so it seemed to me. My mum was. I wasn't. I was more like Leo, a victim of luck, both good and bad. Now I wanted to change, to be more like Beccs, to be doing more for myself, to be more independent. Then perhaps I could start to see Adam as an equal, not just a bringer of more luck, either good or bad.

But not being able to speak to Adam made me want to even more. It would be more acceptable, I told myself, if he'd call me. So I spent half the night looking at my sullen, silent mobile, willing it to ring, willing Adam to call me, as he'd called me so often in the past. It seemed that willing it to happen prevented it. That was how it felt, anyway, when my phone persisted in its resolute silence all through the evening and into the night, pervading even the wordlessness between my mum and me on our way to Solar next morning.

'Ray's expecting me,' my mum said to a new receptionist, as we went in. 'I need to speak to him alone for a while,' she said, inside. 'You go into the studios. I won't be long.'

She wasn't wrong, either. In just a few minutes – in which time the silence of the deserted studios, reinforced by my mobile phone's inactivity, thundered in my ear like a spiteful whisper – she was back with me.

Let me tell you, my mum hardly ever lost her temper. But now she was the closest to it I had ever seen. She was flushed and livid, with a tensed jaw. Her teeth were gritted as she told me we were leaving. I couldn't say anything, following behind as we exited the building, saying nothing to the receptionist, who, because she was new, was still unaccustomed to being treated badly. I tried to nod and smile at her on the way out. It wasn't her fault. She'd probably thought that working in the music industry would be fun. She blinked at me. I would have spoken to her, but words wouldn't come.

We walked away without looking back. It wasn't until we were safely in the back of a black cab, not in any of the Solar-hired vehicles, did my mum give vent to her frustration. 'That man!' she gritted, spitting.

Honestly, I'd never, ever seen her so angry, even when my

dad had lost his last job and spent most of their savings on bills without telling her. She was trembling.

'He's a – he's a –'

'He's a megalomaniac,' I said.

'Exactly! The man's a megalomaniac. He's – he's – I know some of the things you've told me about him – I've – it's –'

She was practically speechless.

'All right, Amy?' the cabbie decided to say, at that moment.

'Oh,' I said. 'Hello.'

'Thought it was you,' he said. 'How's it going?'

I glanced at my mum. She at me. 'It's going – fine,' I managed to say.

The cabbie looked round at us, wearing a pained expression on his face as he looked at my mum.

She and I looked at each other again. My mum could see I was going to laugh, just as I could see she was just about to. We burst out, relieving the tension as much as finding anything funny. We laughed out loud, with lots of love. How we laughed.

The cabbie had to join in with us. It's impossible to be around such laughter without being infected. 'I'm glad it's all going so well,' he said, raising his voice to be heard.

We roared.

'This is my new mobile telephone,' Adam announced, proudly. 'It's for you only.'

'For me?'

'Nobody else. Nobody knows. This is my phone for you. Only you.'

For a moment I couldn't speak. There were lots of things I wanted to say, but my mouth stopped working. I think I gasped. Maybe not. Maybe, though. I breathed, trying to keep myself together, to keep my flyaway emotions reined in.

'I don't believe you,' I said, kind of joking, kind of not.

'You don't believe me?'

'You've gone and got a phone, just for me?'

'Of course. Amy, believe me. Whatever I say, I won't tell lies to you. I won't do that.'

It's something – it is really something when someone says that, when that someone is someone like Adam and – and it brings back all the things I'd been so hurt by in the past, but overcomes them somehow. It's as if those things in the past are there to make these things in the present more important, more real.

'I'm glad I have this telephone,' he was saying, speaking in a phone-line whisper.

I could picture him in Paris, shielding his mobile with an open hand held over his mouth. 'So am I,' I said.

'Yes,' he said. 'Nobody needs to know.'

'Know? Know what?'

'How we speak.'

How we speak? What was so secret about the way in which Adam and I spoke to each other? 'How do we speak?' I said.

'No,' he whispered, 'that we do. We should not. Should we not?'

'Adam,' I said, 'I'm not sure I understand what you're talking about?'

'No,' said Adam, slightly. 'I'm sorry. Maybe you do not understand so well what is happening. I am, forbidden – yes, forbidden to talk to you.'

'Forbidden?'

'Forbidden. It is the right word, I think.'

'Do you think so? You're not allowed to even talk to me?'

'That's it. Not allowed. So they say.'

'Who says?'

'Your people, to my people. We are not allowed, you and I. So I'm glad I have my secret telephone. I must keep it – we must keep it a secret, yes?'

'We've got to keep it a secret? Surely – do your people – does Pierre agree? We can't even talk to each other?'

'It isn't Pierre. It is a legal thing. There is maybe litigation. That is the right word – litigation. We perhaps all go to the courts.'

'What for?'

'Oh, contracts. It is complicated. We must keep us a secret.'

'Us?'

'You and me? Us?'

'Are we an us?'

'Oh, Amy, I would like to think it to be so. What can I say about you and me? Can I say us? Amy? Can I?'

However cross, annoyed, upset I felt about being denied contact with Adam, being included in 'us' with him flattered, flustered, excited me more. I should have been having a Dad-type rant, I knew, but Adam did something else to me, inside. Dangerous stuff, but denying me contact with him only made me want to live more dangerously, to have the very thing I was supposed to have been denied. Control.

'What does it mean,' I said, 'if we're an "us"? Where will that take us?'

'I don't know,' Adam said. 'So many places, possibly. Maybe everywhere. Who knows? I'm – I have to say to you – I am wanting to see you. I have to see you, Amy.'

I touched the necklace he'd given me for my birthday. 'I'm touching lapis lazuli,' I said.

'Are you touching me then?' he whispered.

Oh, oh my – but he was touching me! 'Yes,' I whispered back. 'I hope you can hear me?'

'Yes,' he said.

'Yes,' I said again.

Oh, yes.

I felt afraid. I felt wonderful. I felt stupid. Wise. Generous. Selfish. I hated. I loved. I wanted to cry. I laughed. I touched lapis lazuli. I was touched. Oh, beautiful, beautiful. Adam's words. That's what he said, that what he called me. That's how I felt. I was beautiful.

Ray Ray was ugly. I wanted nothing to do with that ugliness, in case it interfered with the way I was feeling at this moment.

My mum and dad had been talking things over, but had now stopped. Our house settled down with the twins in bed, with a TV set on downstairs where my dad sat, where my mum sat with him, I hoped. I wasn't sure. Whenever my mum got serious about things she became withdrawn. I knew she'd deal with the latest Solar storms for me, but in doing so might isolate herself, especially from my dad.

But none of it seemed to matter very much. When I went to bed that night I was aching to see Adam. When I woke in the morning, the same feeling. It was a good ache. Everything I'd worried about over Adam, the possibility of being used again by someone in the music industry, had evaporated; he was on my side. He agreed that I should have more control over my work and my life. Being involved with Adam was not going to mean being controlled by him. I had begun to trust him not to hurt me.

# ✶✶✶ Nine

**I** spoke to Adam again in the morning. He called me while I was still in bed. When my phone went, I knew instantly that it was him. 'You have slept well, yes?'

'I have,' I said. 'Have you?'

'No,' he said.

'No?'

'Too much on my mind.'

'That happens to me,' I said, 'a lot.'

'No,' he said, 'I think not like this. You do not have you on your mind all night, do you?'

I smiled at him, hoping he could feel it. 'No,' I said, 'but I've been doing a lot of thinking about you.'

'You have? That's good.'

'I need to see you,' I said.

'So I you. Yes. When can we?'

'As soon as possible.'

'I can come to London, in a few days. The train from Paris. It takes no time.'

'Then come to London. I'll meet you, away from prying eyes.'

'We must see each other, though, yes?'

'Yes.'

'We are the same? We are we?'

'Maybe. We'll see. We must be careful.'

'Yes, we must be careful.'

'You must be careful,' my mum warned, before I left that morning. 'You have to go there, but keep out of Ray's way, if you can. Let's just give him a few days to cool off, then I'll go back in. Try to keep your head down till then.'

'*Destination Anywhere!*' Ben said, as soon as he saw me. He was talking about the lyrics of a song I'd written and given to him. I could see he'd been waiting to speak to me about it.

'Static Cats first,' I said. 'Where are they?'

'They're fine. Listen. I've been doing some stuff with them on your song. I like it.'

'You do? You really like it?' This was the first time I'd tried to write anything. Adam had inspired me to do it. 'Are you just saying that?'

'Course not. I really like it.'

'Ben, that's –'

'The Cats like it, too.'

'Have you written a tune for it?'

'Yeah. Easy. The song wrote itself. All the best songs are like that. I've got a rough recording of it if you want to hear what it's –'

'A recording? Already? How?'

'I know a man,' he said. He sounded like his old self, the Ben I first knew at school, bright with ideas and confidence. The old Ben always 'knew a man', always had a contact, a way of getting things done.

'A man?'

'He has a little studio. In his house. A friend of mine. No shortage of singers. Three of them, to be precise.'

'The Cats,' I said.

'Want to hear it?'

Did I want to hear it? My own lyrics turned into a song and sung by three performers as good as the Static Cats? I couldn't wait.

We borrowed a studio and Ben whipped out the CD he was carrying in an inside pocket and quickly stuck it into the machine, as if the disk itself should not be seen. 'It's just a rough,' he said. 'Don't expect too much.'

I didn't. In fact, I expected a whole lot less than I got. The song started on just a few beats, before one of the Cats sang, *'Oh, yeah!'*

'Oh, yeah!' I said.

Ben smiled.

*Hurry up, hurry up*
*We ain't got much time.*
*I got my motor gunning*
*Like I'm doing Car Crime.*

I smiled now. Ben had changed the lyric to include the Car Crime reference. He was looking at me to see if I minded, but my smile gave him his answer.

The song went on:

*Tired of sittin' waitin'*
*'S gettin' all too much.*
*Feel like grinding thru my gears.*
*Feel like burning my clutch.*

*Revvin' in my brain (good to go)*
*Rhythm in my veins (so let me know)*
*Driving me insane (you ready to roll?)*

74

The Cats were taking it in turns to sing, with all three joining in at the end of each line. The chorus came:

*We're going nowhere,*
*But lookin' good while we get there.*
*So follow if you dare,*
*to destination anywhere.*
*We're both out on a roll, runnin' out of control,*
*Hold me, don't let me go!*

'Ben,' I said, 'this is a great song!'

Leo came in at that point to see what we were up to. 'Leo,' I said, 'listen to this. Listen to this! Ben, start it again so Leo can hear it from the beginning.'

We all listened to it run through. I could see by the look on Leo's face how much he liked it.

*So follow if you dare,*
*To destination anywhere.*
*We're both out on a roll,*
*  runnin' out of control,*
*Hold me, don't let me go!*
*Yeah! Yeah!*

'Oh, yeah!' I shouted. 'Turn it up! Turn it up! I love it!'

*Come with me, run with me,*
*Laugh and have fun with me,*
*Tell me now, what do you say?*
*There's nowhere to hide with me,*
*Take a joy ride with me,*
*Nothing can stand in our way!*

At that point, Ben had inserted the sound of a car, accelerating. The car took off, shifting gear, doing the speed-of-excitement, or excitement-of-speed thing that Ben had always wanted in his music.

'Oh, yes!' I cried.

Leo laughed, he liked it so much.

Ray said nothing. Yet. We didn't know he was there, standing by the door, listening. Watching. Waiting.

'Where did this come from?' Leo asked.

'Yes,' Ray's voice came at us. 'Where from?'

The music stopped immediately. Ben cut it as soon as he saw Ray, the expression on Ray's face, the colour-coded messaging system of his mood expressions.

For a moment, none of us found anything to say. My mum had advised me, as I left that morning, to keep my head down: down it fell.

'Speak!' Ray spoke.

'Ray –' Leo started.

'Not you! I want to know what you want to know. Where from? This stuff? What is it?'

'We wrote it,' Ben said.

'We?'

'Me. Amy.'

Ray's attention clicked from one position, from one person to the next. It alighted on me, dreadfully quick and all of a sudden. 'You? How you?'

'She –' Ben tried.

Ray held up a hand. 'Amy!'

'I wrote the lyrics,' I said.

'What for?'

The question halted me. It came so unexpectedly. It sounded very much like a challenge. 'What for?' I said.

'Ray,' Leo said again, only to be halted once more, silenced by the challenge of Ray's face snapping another all-of-a-sudden glare in his direction. His attention snapped from one to the other of us, Leo, Ben and me, as we stood guiltily accused of a crime we hadn't realised we were committing.

'What,' Ray said to me, deliberately, 'are you doing? Lyrics? I haven't sanctioned this.'

'No,' I said, 'but why shouldn't I?'

The air seemed to be shocked, to be shuddering all round us as Ray emanated his hate energy from the other side of the room. 'You,' he said. He stopped. He breathed, sucking in the shocked air as if to try to deny us a breath.

'There's too much of this,' he said. His teeth were horribly gritted. More grit was in his eyes. 'What's happening – too much! Too much!'

He glared at Ben.

'Take it easy, boss,' Ben said.

He glared at me.

I glared back. 'I want more control,' I said.

Ray breathed.

The grit in the air clogged my lungs. 'I want more say in what happens. I want –'

'You want!' he roared. 'You want! Who are you? Wants! Who the hell!'

'Take it easy, boss.'

'Shut your mouth, boy! You!' he yelled at Leo. 'Get out! Did you hear me? I said get out! Why aren't you going?'

'Ray, calm down. Don't –'

'Control?' Ray bellowed at me. 'You want control? Meaning what?'

I merely opened my mouth to speak.

'Shut it!' he shouted. 'Control? Control? Trying to write songs to write me out! Is that it?'

'No, I –'

'Calling up those French on secret phones, is that it?'

'No! Wait! How did you –'

'I have control!' Ray crowed, pale-faced and grey-lipped. 'I know everything. That's what it means, having control. It means –'

'It means searching through my stuff and interfering with my phone!' I yelled back.

Ray dashed forward, stamping. He pointed at Leo. 'You! Get out!' Then at Ben. 'And you!'

'Take it easy, boss.'

'You'd better get gone, boy.'

'Ray –'

'Now! Now! Why aren't you – you'll get gone for good, hear me? Boy? You're fired! You understand?'

Ben's face had gone pale, too. Leo took him by the arm.

'Don't hold him!' Ray shouted. 'Let him come at me, if that's what he wants. Is that what you want, boy?'

'Don't say anything, Ben,' I said.

Leo was still holding onto him.

'I want you out!' Ray screamed at him. He turned to Leo. 'You get him out, you understand? Do it! And you –' he pointed at me – 'you're to phone France. Tell that – that – tell *him* it's finished! Hear me? All of you? Hear me? Hear me! I'm talking, you listen! Hear me? Hear me!'

We could hear him. Oh, we could all hear him, including Big Ron, the studio manager, who seemed to simply amble in at that moment, saying nothing, looking calmly from one to the other of us, assuring us, all of us, that we would keep calm.

Even Ray was afraid of Ron. I could see, or rather sense the wariness tempering Ray's temper, cooling him down, so that his face whitened still further until it was like the mask of a Japanese geisha.

'Will you go to my office and wait for me?' Ray seethed at me.

I looked at Leo then Ben. I shook my head. 'No,' I said. Nothing more.

'Are you going?' he said to Leo.

Leo shook his curly locks.

Ray faltered, facing mutiny. 'You're going,' he said, at length, to Ben. 'You are going, boy. I'll have you out. And you two too, if you're not careful.' He glanced at Ron. 'Be careful,' he said to us. 'Be very careful.'

He left then, walking slowly, deliberately. We could all see how much he was shaking. Every move he made trembled, almost like a resonation of the air.

When he'd gone, Ron looked at us all in turn. Then he went, saying nothing. We also said nothing. We all left and went home, without speaking, to anyone. That was the end to it. It was all over.

# ✳✳✳ Ten

**N**o more Raymond Raymond? No more Solar control over my life? Could it be that this was the end to my pop music career?

This was so scary! You were either with Ray, or you were against him. We both – no, we all understood that: my parents, me, Ray, Leo, Ben, everyone at Solar, and everyone else that had ever had anything at all to do with Ray's empire, the Solar-system of nuclear warmth and light holding in place all the satellite orbits of Ray's acolytes and few friends and all his potential enemies. To be out of this light was to be cast into the darkness. Ray was going to make a strong and formidable foe. It made me feel slightly sick every time I thought about it.

'Don't worry,' my mum said to me, as we discussed what might happen next.

'Are you sure?' my dad sidled up later. 'Are you sure this is what you want?'

'No,' I said. 'Dad, I'm not sure what I want. I don't want any more hurt or harm, that's all. It isn't what I want, it's what I don't want I'm thinking about.'

He tried to understand. He couldn't do it, but he did his best. The twins laughed as he stood on his head for them. They were fascinated by his upside-down mouth as he talked. 'The world sometimes looks better like this,' he said.

'Sometimes it makes everything look the right way up. You should try it sometimes,' he said to my mum.

To everyone's delight, she grabbed a cushion and stood on her head next to him; the two of them side by side against the wall, with the twins running backwards and forwards, laughing and screaming and doing little forward rolls on the living room carpet.

Then Mum and Dad were down, both red in the face, collapsing on the carpet with the twins jumping on top of them.

'Ames,' my dad said, holding out an arm to me. 'Come here.'

He held me with one arm, my mum with the other, with the girls tumbling on top of us all. There we were, a whole heap of Peppercorns on the floor, the bunch of us one of the same thing: a family.

'Oh, so you can come to Paris again,' Adam said, as soon as I told him what had happened and what it probably meant. 'Get away from everything, for a little while only. Why can't you?'

I was going to say 'I can't', but Adam pre-empted me by asking why not. 'I can't,' I said, anyway.

'But why?'

'There are going to be things going on here. My mum's going to consult a lawyer to see what might happen with my contract, all that.'

'All that? It's nothing. Come here. One day. Come in the morning, go home tonight – not tonight. That night. You do not have to stay. You will be safe. Amy, you are safe with me.'

I laughed.

'What is it?' Adam said.

He couldn't see the tears I could see sparkling in my eyes. I had to be careful, very, very careful. Speaking to me like that, I had to laugh, or I'd have cried. It's always like that with me, the way my emotions come up after the event. Things happen, I seem to deal with them, then experience, or more like suffer the emotional consequences afterwards. Splitting with Solar, getting away from Ray like that had somehow seemed quite exciting, in a weird and scary way, at first. Then the doubts and the fears set in, so hard that I started to feel more and more sick. I couldn't sleep; that always happened. This was it! This was actually it! What could I do with myself now, if it was all over?

Adam being so nice, so lovely to me, did nothing for my resolve to be strong and not to worry. I had to laugh, or I'd have cried. 'It's nothing,' I said.

'No,' he said, 'it's not nothing. You are upset. You must be. I must not try to make you –'

'No,' I said. 'No, it's fine. Make me, Adam. Make me, or I'll sit here and stew in my own juices. There's nothing I can do. You're right. I'll come. Tomorrow?'

His turn to laugh now. 'Oh, no. Not tomorrow. I have such a day.'

'Of course. I'm sorry.'

'No. Not sorry. Don't be. Please. In two days, come to Paris. I will love to see you.'

'Yes,' I said, 'and I will love to see you, too.'

'Beccs,' I whispered, 'oh, my friend, where are you? Why are you always so deep in study, or else asleep?'

As soon as I whispered it to myself, I regretted being so selfish. She was studying like mad, I knew. I'd be all right, so would she. We were . . .

'Stop questioning everything,' I had to say to myself. 'Stop it and go to sleep.'

'Stop it and go to sleep,' I was saying to myself the next night, then the next. Being at home was going to drive me nuts. I was supposed to make an appearance at a Solar function and do a couple of interviews, but everything was probably cancelled, so I didn't bother going. I sat around doing nothing. Beccs was at school, study group, football practice, home, bed. She sent me this text in response to one I sent her: 'Can we talk at the weekend? I am struggling to fit everything in. Can't seem to get enough sleep. Can you give me a few days?'

Written in longhand like that, it didn't seem at all as if Beccs had sent it. She was a texter, a word abbreviationist. But her messages were coming through sounding almost like they'd been written by somebody else, as if they'd been dictated. She seemed strange, but then I supposed I did too, always leaving her long messages listing all my woes.

I texted her: 'off 2 paris 2moro. cu v. soon. all lv. a. xxx.'

Ray came through in his own kind of abbreviated words, or so my mum told me. Apparently, he'd been on demanding to know where I was.

'She's here,' my mum told him.

'I'll speak to her,' he said.

'No, you won't.'

'You what?'

'You'll not speak to her.'

'Where was she this afternoon? She was supposed –'

'We know where she was supposed to be. Ray, I'm talking to a lawyer about this.'

'What? About what?'

He tried to sound as if he didn't know or understand what was bothering us. He tried that – when it didn't work, he went ape, going ballistic over the phone at my mum again, accusing her, calling her names. I don't know what. All I know is that it was bad, judging by my mum's reaction.

'I think he's losing it,' she said, coming off the phone. She was quite pale, nervous, if not frightened. No, I think she was frightened. She was experiencing at first hand just how frightening Ray could be, even over the telephone.

My dad was silent. He couldn't understand it, any of it. But there was nothing more he could say, especially seeing his wife so disturbed. He and the twins were each looking at her as if they had never quite seen her before.

'This is going to get ugly,' she said, quietly, more to herself than anyone else.

My dad got up and went and stood in front of her. 'You're right,' he said.

'I wish I wasn't,' she said.

'No, I mean about the whole thing.' He glanced at me. But mostly he was watching her, my mum, his wife. 'Jill,' he said, 'you are absolutely right.'

The twins were incredibly quiet; they had also seen how right my mum was and what it all meant, by the look on her face after that phone call from Ray. Jo and George watched their nice dad take their mum in his arms. They didn't do anything, the girls, but sat in silence; so I went and hugged them in gratitude for their sensitivity and understanding. They responded by hitting me on the head of course, which was only to be expected and was a relief when we all laughed.

I looked at my mum. She at me. Our eyes exchanged all we needed to know from each other: Ray Ray could do nothing against us, not with my dad and the twins and all of us laughing and smiling together. Ray had nothing compared to what we had, nothing. Oh, he could destroy my pop career, but he couldn't damage my family. Against that, he was powerless.

A text came through from Angel Iago, telling she and the Cats were doing fine. I couldn't text her back yet. Advised to contact no one for the time being, I had to whisper to my mum where I was going and why. For a moment I thought she would forbid me to go to Paris to see Adam, but only for a moment. She faltered, her eyes flickering once, before she smiled and touched my arm and leaned forward to whisper to me. 'Whatever you do, don't let your father know where you're going. Not yet. I'll tell him, when the time's right.'

My mum always told my dad the truth, just not the whole of it all at once. His truths had to come at him in instalments, so as not to worry or distract him from his main task. He looked after the twins, while my mum took care of me.

So it was without full parental approval that I got off the fast train in Paris that morning. Believe it or not, and I could hardly believe it myself, but this was the first time I'd travelled abroad on my own. Looking back on past appearances in Europe, and the little tour of radio stations I'd done in the States, it seemed as if I'd been to some of these places on my own. But no, I had always been accompanied, chaperoned. Until now.

The train station was huge, but Adam would have known which platform I was due to arrive at. I was in Paris to meet him and he wasn't there!

Then he was. There he was, so suddenly, going from not being there to being there, I felt my breathing falter as my eyes swam for a moment and that feeling – that feeling! – welled up from the pit of my stomach. He was a pop star! A French pop star was waiting for me on Gare du Nord looking like – he looked like a French pop star. Obviously! But what if I were no longer a British pop star? What then? And what would he think of me? What would I be? I'd just be a silly girl, coming here like this, getting in the way. Adam was there, coming towards me, but I felt as if I was shrinking in front of him, in front of his unquestionable pop-stardom, his talent, his real good looks.

'You are here!' he declared, walking straight up to me. He kissed me, one cheek, about to kiss the other.

But we stopped, midway, kind of thing, face to face. Adam was wondering whether or not to kiss me properly. I was wondering whether to let him. I didn't. I just stopped wondering and kissed him first. 'I'm here,' I smiled, trying to appear more confident than I really felt.

'I am glad. Very glad. Amy is here. You have come to Paris because I asked you to. I asked you, and you came.'

'Yes. I did want to get away. But I feel sort of – strange.'

'You have such trouble at home now, so here is very good for you.'

'I hope so.'

We had started walking along the platform. Adam was holding me by the arm; a funny gesture I'd never seen before – the other way round, yes. It would have felt safe, if I hadn't been feeling quite so imperilled.

'You are hungry, after your journey?'

'No. Thirsty. Shall we get a drink?'

'Yes. Shall we go to PPF?'

'PPF?'

'Yes. I would very much like you to see our studios. You haven't been there.'

I still really liked the way he told me things like that: I hadn't been to PPF. Adam said it as if I wouldn't have realised I'd never been there had he not told me. I laughed. 'I haven't been there,' I had to agree.

'So we should go, no?'

'I'm not sure, Adam. Meeting you is one thing. Going to PPF is entirely another. I feel like – things are going all wrong. All sorts of bad things are about to happen – legal procedures.'

'Oh, it's okay. Pierre understands about legal procedures. He has many friends.'

'That must be wonderful,' I said, 'having many friends. Pierre is a very, very nice man.'

'Yes, he is. He is your friend, too.'

'Mine?'

'Yes.'

'Adam,' I said, 'what if I'm no longer a – it scares me – what if my singing career's over? I'm so – I thought I was going to be stronger about it. But I'm not. What if it's all over? It could be, you know.'

'If it is?'

'What will happen to me? Will Pierre be my friend then? Will you?'

He stopped us. He turned to me. 'Do you think I want to see you, do you think I want to see you because you are a pop singer?'

'I don't know.'

'Do you not think I know many, many pop singers, many girls, singers, stars? Do you think I want to kiss them all?'

'I think perhaps you might,' I smiled, although the thought didn't really make me feel like smiling. I just did it because Adam was in front of me, looking so serious. 'I don't know,' I smiled. 'Perhaps you might. I don't know.'

He was so lovely, you see. How can you trust such looks, such confidence, such charm? How can you believe in it? Especially believing it was all for you, for me rather; that it was concentrated on me and me alone? When I wasn't there – with Adam I mean – was he really not using his looks, his confidence and stardom, practising his charm on all those others he confessed to knowing?

When we went for a drink together – the way the girls, the women, the French ladies all looked at him. They knew who he was, of course. But then they looked at me, with a cursory kind of glance that wasn't exactly friendly. I couldn't help thinking that yes, Adam had kissed them all and forgotten about it – but they hadn't! And they all looked so – so French! Which was like comfortably casual, but right up there with the fashion. I felt, sort of as if my clothes were wearing me, as if I wasn't so right for fashion as these comfortably cool French girls.

We jumped in a taxi to go to the Champs-Élysées. The traffic on the big roundabout on the Arc de Triomph was breathtaking, like a white-knuckle ride through masses of cars all moving and milling with no apparent system to stop them driving into each other. Not that I'd have been able to determine a system, with my eyes closed most of the time. Somehow or other we made it through unscathed and were set down on the pavement where we chose a café for coffee where Adam seemed to know everyone. He knew no one of course. They knew him. The French girls did, every one.

We sat and had strong coffee and water and watched people passing. 'From here, it is only a walk to PPF. We must go, yes? We must. I have someone I would very much like you to meet.'

'Really? Who is she?' That 'she' sounded silly and lacking in confidence and – and jealous. I couldn't help it. Adam was the star, not me. I was just another passer-by, flicking a glance at him every now and then, afraid to look right at him in case something good or something bad happened. Either way, I was wary of what it might be.

Adam smiled. 'Oh, it is not she. It is he. You will like him. I can guarantee it.'

'You can guarantee it?'

'Oh, yes.'

'How can you be so sure?'

'Ah. I know some things.'

'Things?'

'About you. I understand about you.'

'Do you?' I said. I understood practically nothing about Adam. All the things I wanted to ask him about himself, his family, his background, his interests, all seemed stifled in me simply because I was afraid to seem too interested. 'What do you understand about me?'

'Oh, about what you like – about what you are like. About

when we have walked by the river. About lapis lazuli. When we have danced. The things you like. I understand.'

I couldn't help it; I leaned forward in my chair, across the table to give him a kiss. His charm cast its spell, and I fell.

He kissed me too. On the pavement on a chilly and overcast day on the Champs-Élysées, we kissed like a couple. The girls on the next table, where they had all been looking and looking, were gazing away in the other direction after that kiss. Something must have distracted them. I couldn't see what it was. Neither, I suspected, could they.

PIERRE PIATTA FANTASTIQUE. It was written on the window. We were in a street of small galleries with pictures and sculptures and photographs, tiny bistros and small select clothes outlets. It was all very fashionable and young, but elegant in a casual way, very exciting and energetic; in contrast to the exhausted main street on which Solar was situated, looking like a converted car showroom. PPF appeared to be another gallery at first glance, with wildly colourful carpets and relaxed sofas on which it looked perfectly possible to completely unwind. There were stands with sweets on them. The pictures at the exhibition inside were all of artists and records or CD covers, silver, gold and platinum discs, signed photos of stars and celebs from France and Britain and America. There were world-renowned R & B artists pictured, with felt-tip messages of thanks to Pierre and the team at PPF.

'Wow!' I said. 'Do you know all these people?'

Adam laughed. 'No. Only some.'

'But surely all these artists – the Americans – they're not with PPF, are they?'

'Mostly no. Just some. A few. Mostly, Pierre helps in Europe, you understand?'

There was no reception at PPF, only a door buzzer, which, for known people like Adam, opened immediately, directly into the gallery area. A few people were concentrating on computers. An astoundingly beautiful girl bustled by, popping a lollipop into her mouth as if to intimidate me. The way I felt, everything seemed to want to intimidate me. But Adam spoke to and introduced me to absolutely everybody. My head was buzzing with all the different names.

Music was playing. Above it, and above our heads, my own name was being called. 'Amy! Amy Peppercorn!'

Adam pointed up to a smoked glass petition at the top of an open staircase at the far end of the gallery.

'Amy Peppercorn!' Pierre was calling over a kind of glass balcony. 'Welcome. Come up. Please, come up.' Pierre greeted me like an old friend. 'Good to see you again. You look good. Adam, she looks good.'

Adam nodded his assent as I laughed and blushed.

'We wanted you to come,' Pierre said.

'We?' I said, glancing at Adam.

'Oh,' Pierre said, 'Adam did, I know. I didn't ask him, he told me you were coming. I wanted to see you, anyway. Sit down, please. Adam, you too. Amy, speak with me. How is your manager?'

I breathed. 'Oh, I'm not sure I should be –'

'No. Quite right. Quite right. You do not need to say. I know. He is a strange man, is he not? Yes, I think. You do not need to say. But there is much trouble at your company. We have it that you are seeking to leave.'

He waited. He hadn't actually asked me a question, so I waited too.

'So,' he said, after a pause. 'Raymond Raymond is not so

happy. This is for sure. He is maybe a little crazy? Yes, maybe. It will be made much easier for you, I think.'

'Much easier?'

'He is – what is it – unworkable? If you can prove him so – who can work with such a man? Oh, but I'm sure your lawyers – you have lawyers?'

'My mum's dealing with it.'

'Ah, good. Your mother. Good. We would like – Adam especially – would like to show our studios. Our work in progress?'

'And I'd like to see them.'

'Then I'll leave you to – Adam will show you, yes, Adam? Then perhaps we should take lunch together, all of us?'

'What about the someone you wanted me to meet?' I said to Adam as we went down the open staircase.

On our way down more stairs to the basement, Adam said, 'You will meet him. You will like him, very much.'

I laughed. 'I wish I knew how you can be so sure. It's very quiet,' I said. 'There's not much going on.'

'More than you think,' Adam said, cryptically. 'No, not that studio. We are in the end one.'

'We are?'

'Amy,' he said, taking me by the hand, turning me towards him. 'Stop, one moment. I haven't done this, although I wanted it to happen.'

'What? Wanted what to happen?'

'Oh, so much. This,' he said, just before kissing me gently on the cheek. 'And this,' on the other cheek. He held my eyes with his. 'And, this?' he half questioned, touching my lips with his. 'And,' he said again, touching my mouth again, more firmly with his. 'You are very special,' he whispered.

How could I – what was I supposed to do? I was powerless

to resist. 'Am I?' I whispered back. 'Am I, Adam?' I wanted to be special, especially now.

'Very special,' he said, softly.

'Adam, I need to be. I can't do this otherwise. This, or anything else. I need to be sure.'

'How can we be sure of anything? Nothing is sure, is it?'

'Some things are. If we're going to – if you and I are . . .'

'I hope we are. I do.'

'If we do,' I said, 'then you can be sure of me. And I'll need to feel sure of you. That's as sure as we can be.'

'We can be, I think.'

He wanted to kiss me again. 'Wait,' I said. 'I need to ask you this: why me?'

'Why you?'

'Yes. Of all the girls you could – why me? Why not the Cats? Angel? Why not Miranda? She's gorgeous. She likes you, I know she does.'

'Amy,' he said, gently.

'What, is it because I'm – what if I'm not a pop star any more? What if I'm just me?'

'You are just you. That's all. That's good.'

'Is it? Just me?'

'Just you,' he said, trying to kiss me again. Succeeding. Kissing me. 'Just you,' he whispered again.

'I think I'm going to trust you,' I said. 'I don't know why. Why am I?'

'Because,' he said. Then said nothing. He ran his fingers through my hair. He looked at me. That did it. Because would have to be good enough, for now.

'Come on,' he said, taking me by the hand, leading me to the studio at the end of the corridor in which we were standing.

'Here we are,' he said, before opening the door. 'This is

where I wanted you to come. Here,' he said, opening the door to the studio. The door swung aside. 'This is who I wanted you to meet,' as the door opened fully on its hinges.

Inside, they were waiting. They were waiting for me.

# **Eleven**

*Hurry up, hurry up*
*We ain't got much time.*
*I got my motor gunning*
*Like I'm doing Car Crime.*

'Ben! What are you doing here? Ben!' I ran to him, bear-hugging him. What a surprise!

'What a surprise!' I said. 'You're here! And you!' I called to the Static Cats as they appeared as if from nowhere. 'Angel! Kaylie! Miranda! You're all here!' They were all there: fantastically, brilliantly, wonderfully.

Angel was the first to get to me. We hugged like long lost friends. It felt like that. It felt like such a relief.

Then we were in uproar, with the Cats and me screeching at the tops of our voices, with Ben and Adam laughing, with music playing, in my head as well as in the studio.

'Everyone's here!' I shrieked.

'Don't tell her!' Adam shouted. 'Don't tell her! Not yet!'

'Tell me what?'

There was a lot of laughing going on, laughing, smiling, laughing. We were all shouting, doing little bits of dances with each other. I must have hugged Ben ten times and Adam twenty. Ben was a real good friend. Adam, more than that: I kissed him. It was – can you imagine how I felt? After all that had been happening at Solar, the sackings, the bad feelings –

can you imagine how it felt to have everyone here unexpected like this, coming together like old friends glad, so very glad to be seeing one another again?

'I told you you'd like him,' Adam said.

I laughed. 'What is it they're not to tell me?'

'Sing, first,' Adam said, nodding at Ben.

The music to my song, the one I'd written with Ben, *Destination Anywhere*, had been playing all along. Now Ben stopped it using a remote control, starting it again at the beginning. The girls, the Static Cats started to sing it.

'Come on!' Ben yelled at me.

We all knew the words. They were my words. The Cats had memorised them:

*I got my motor gunning*
*Like I'm doing Car Crime.*

*Tired of sittin' waitin'*
*'S gettin' all too much.*
*Feel like grinding through my gears.*
*Feel like burning my clutch.*

Pierre came in at this point, smiling and nodding at us all, standing next to Adam, watching what we were all doing.

We were singing, dancing. Straight away we were having such a good time.

*Revvin' in my brain (good to go)*
*Rhythm in my veins (so let me know)*
*Driving me insane (you ready to roll?)*

Pierre was watching as we sang, taking turns, harmonising, singing in ones, twos, threes and fours.

*We're going nowhere,*
*But lookin' good while we get there.*
*So follow if you dare,*
*To destination anywhere!*
*We're both out on a roll, runnin' out of control,*
*Hold me, don't let me go!*

It was funny, but sounded good at the same time. We were having a great time. All of a sudden Paris didn't seem like a city in a foreign country. It felt as if we should be here, all of us.

*We're going nowhere,*
*But lookin' good while we get there.*
*So follow if you dare,*
*To destination anywhere!*

'Car Crime! Destination everywhere!' Ben called out. 'This is good, isn't it?'

The Static Cats agreed with him, obviously. So did I, but didn't quite understand as well as they all seemed to. Adam appeared beside me, touching me on the arm.

'We should have lunch,' Pierre said, extending his arms. 'All have lunch, and we shall see.'

'I see,' I said.

Ben was bouncing. Angel and Kaylie and Miranda were throwing things at him and laughing. 'This is it!' Ben was saying, shielding himself from flying screwed-up napkins and pieces of breadsticks. 'The Static Cats are willing to wail as part of it.' A piece of hard bread caught him on the cheek and Kaylie lingeringly kissed it better.

'It will mean some trouble,' Adam said.

'But you have trouble already,' said Pierre. 'This is not going to make it worse for you. For me, perhaps. For you, no.'

'You will work,' said Adam.

'It will work,' Ben said.

'You'll work with us,' said Angel.

'Car Crime!' said Ben again.

My head was spinning with everyone's voices chipping in. Apparently, my song *Destination Anywhere* was going to be first on my new album. I was going to be working closely with a new band.

'Car Crime!'

'But I –'

'I have copies of a new interim contract,' Pierre said.

'How?'

He smiled. Adam smiled and took my hand. The Cats smiled. They grinned.

'It is a way around your problems,' Pierre said.

'You can go everywhere – all Europe,' said Adam.

'Europe?'

'I have arranged it,' Pierre said. 'But you will need other songs. I have never done such a thing.'

'Pierre believes in you,' Adam said.

'We can write the songs,' said Ben.

Miranda kissed Ben then. So Kaylie kissed him again.

'This is madness,' I said. 'When? Where in Europe? When?'

'Two weeks,' said Adam.

I sat stunned. Everyone was laughing.

'We have some songs,' Pierre said.

'So do we,' Ben said to me. 'Car Crime. Remember? We can do it now. Now we can do it.'

'But, there isn't time.'

'You must not go home,' Adam said. He squeezed my hand under the table. 'You must stay in Paris.'

'But my mum –'

'She will come,' Pierre said. 'She will come to Paris, she says. In two days, maybe three.'

'But I don't have – we don't have –'

'We've got everything,' Ben said.

'I don't even have a change of clothes!'

'Clothes?' Pierre said. 'This is Paris!'

'Clothes!' – Angel.

'Make-up!' – Kaylie.

'Hair!' – Miranda.

'This is Paris,' Adam said.

I was looking round the table at everyone in turn. 'I don't believe this,' I said.

'You will be Car Crime,' Pierre said. 'You will be Amy Peppercorn and Car Crime, featuring the Static Cats. All together, with Ben, and maybe one, maybe two others, you will be Car Crime.'

'We will be Car Crime!' I said. I raised my glass. There was only water in it, but the gesture was right.

'We'll be Car Crime!' declared Ben and the Cats, raising their glasses.

'Car Crime!' – from Adam and Pierre.

Car Crime! And we were once again committed to it, both Ben and I, as we smiled, survivors, committing our crimes, and getting away with them all over again.

I couldn't believe it! Who would have? One minute I was sick with worry, unable to think about my career – the next, bang! Suddenly I was onto the most manic and crazy and exciting time of my whole life. This was it, you see, for me. In one day I'd gone from probably having the pop-carpet pulled from under me, to landing on my feet looking at another, very different kind of contract. Pierre was taking an awful risk, taking on Ray Ray like this, looking for loopholes in contracts. Why was he doing this?

'He believes in you,' Adam said. 'As I do. Do you believe in me now? I need to know. You will be very busy. We will have little or no time together. What are we together, Amy?'

'Together we're together,' I said. 'Apart, I don't know. What can I say about what you do when I'm not there?'

'It is difficult for us, no?'

'It is difficult for us, yes.'

'Too difficult?'

'I don't know.'

'No,' he said. 'No. I don't think so. We are a good combination. That is the right word, I think?'

I laughed. 'Are we?'

'English, French. That is good.'

'Certainly unusual.'

'Yes, that is what we are. We are certainly unusual.'

Then that was what we were: our only certainty, our unusualness. Fine by me. The danger of my new life seemed to beg uncertainty, in all aspects.

Things went crazy. Ben and I started writing songs, putting stuff together, resurrecting some of our old Car Crime material. That felt strange, as if we shouldn't have been going there. We both felt it, but neither of us said anything. We needed the material too much.

Pierre insisted I still had *If Ever*, as it was an old song anyway, and *Never Let You Go*, as it had been written by Adam. Songs, stuff, material, new music was coming at us from every quarter.

I went shopping with the Cats. Oh my, what a time! We went berserk in the Paris designer and high street outlets – high street! We were in the centre of Paris! No high street, but you know what I mean. We went shopping for clothes. Four of us, out together, four English girls in Paris – out for a laugh, but with some purpose and some money in our pockets to buy whatever we wanted. We went everywhere, tried on everything. I went mad for all the little tops they had in all the shops. I wanted to feel like some of the Paris girls looked – in sharp-cut beautiful trousers, those fantastic little tops. Most of the stuff wasn't really any different from all the designer-wear that had been given to me back in England, but looking for it in Paris, trying it on with the Cats was something else. It was fantastic. The best time I'd had, apart from being in live performance on stage, since Beccs and I – Beccs! She'd have loved to have been with us. As soon as I thought about her, I felt guilty for not thinking about her before now. Not that I'd forgotten her, but we were having such a good time, and my head was full of –

'Adam's dead interested in you,' Miranda was saying to me. 'Lucky little –'

We laughed. My head was full of when he'd kissed me the night before. And the things he'd said. 'The things he says!' I said to Miranda.

'I know,' she said.

She was smiling, looking lovely, giving me a strange uneasily sudden shift in my emotions, like a burst of jealousy. We were sitting having a Coke in a café, besieged by bags of mainly my clothes purchases, looking at the people who were looking at us. Angel was looking about at everyone, so was Kaylie. Miranda was still smiling at me. I was wondering what to say next, when two fellas came over wanting to know where we came from.

'We're from everywhere,' Angel said, smiling in that way she did.

We were all English, but Angel's parents were from Sri Lanka, Kaylie's grandparents were Jamaican and Miranda's mum was from London, her dad from Ethiopia. They looked – what was it? – international? Exotic? They looked fantastic. If I thought about it too much, the Cats made me feel kind of ordinary, on my own, set apart from them.

'We're from all over the place,' Miranda said, her eyes flashing, smile broadening.

The French boys had spoken in English. 'But where are you going?' one of them said.

'We're going up,' I cut in, completely shuffling off what Miranda had been making me feel.

'We used to be Static Cats,' Angel glanced at me, smiling warmly. 'But we're not static any more. We're on the move, right, girls? Come on, let's move out of here, for a start.'

The boys didn't understand what we were on about. It didn't matter. We knew. They were still Cats, I was always Amy P, but we were all together in Car Crime. Thank you. We were on the move. New clothes! French shoes! High boots! Individual make-up and hair! Paris provided everything we needed and more. Much more.

Out that evening, the four of us, wearing clothes as if – wearing clothes out as they should be worn, to be seen in. We were seen. We were heard. Nobody could have missed us. Scream? Laugh? Dance? What a time! It was like everything I'd missed out on for so long. It was like being let out of a prison cell, coming from a dark place into the light. Paris was alight with us in it, blazing our way through the stores and cafés and restaurants and clubs. My eyes were glistening, I knew, full up as they were with the many coloured lights of young Paris, this old city in its never-ending youth, its feeling of then and now, and now, and how!

Wow! You should have seen us! We were out, you know? Out. Oh, You, Tee! I was all excitement and relief, almost as if I'd been allowed to have lots of friends again after a long period of hanging on for dear life to what I had with Beccs. That wouldn't be affected, ever, by anything; but I could see now how it didn't have to be all I had. Beccs had other friends, didn't she? Now I had Angel, who seemed to get it, to understand what I was like and what I was about. Beccs was getting harder and harder to get through to, so I was bound to find a friend in Angel, wasn't I?

The other two, Kaylie and Miranda, spent a whole lot of time in competition for Ben's attention. Girls had always done that around Ben. He was cool. Sometimes he seemed more interested in Angel than in either Kaylie or Miranda. But only sometimes.

'That's because I'm not interested in him,' Angel said to me.

The four of us, the Cats and me, were out in our new clothes without Ben or Adam, but we spent a lot of time talking about them. Miranda and Kaylie were showing off on the little dance floor of the bar we were in. They looked fantastic, especially as they were the only two dancing in there at the time.

'I'm not interested in him,' Angel said, because I happened to mention that Ben sometimes seemed quite keen on her. 'He'll get over it. Look at those two,' she said, nodding towards the dance floor, 'attention seekers.'

I laughed. 'We all are, aren't we?'

'Yes,' she said, moving closer to me, shouting into my ear, which was like a whisper under the thunderous volume of the dance music. 'Yes, we are. But I've noticed something. I'm like you,' she said. Her head moved back so we could look at each other. Our heads came back together again. 'We don't like to show it when we like them, do we. Ben, I mean. And Adam. That's what does it.'

'Does it?' I said. We laughed. Then we went and danced with the other two, the four of us showing off like crazy, feeling free, on the verge of something good and very special. Kaylie and Miranda were attention seekers, yes, but so were we all. The way we were dancing! Four girls – all of us, together.

Well, almost together: Angel was like me; she was right. We both loved to dance and to show off in that way, but we were more self-contained when it came to – well, to Ben, and Adam, when it came to deeper emotions. As we danced, all four of us, as we just enjoyed ourselves, Angel and I would dance together every now and then, as would the other two. We all felt it, falling into it quite naturally. Angel was more with me and I with her, as Kaylie and Miranda were more together, even though they pretended to fight for Ben's affection. Or not pretending. Whichever.

It didn't matter. Nothing matters when you're having such a good time, does it?

Angel and I were sharing a room. The hotel was quite small, and such a refreshingly far cry from the anonymous chain of rooms I'd dwelt in on previous tours and in America. We were in one of those little back streets in Paris that look so lovely: lots of tiny balconies with wrought iron looking out over the street. It was almost possible to jump from our balcony onto the one on the building opposite.

'I'd like to try it,' I said. 'You know, like those people that jump from one bit of a building onto another. Have you seen them? They're mad.'

'Cool, though,' Angel said.

'Oh, yeah,' I agreed. 'Fit, too.'

'You know, I didn't think you were like this,' Angel said, smiling.

'Like what?'

'You know. Like you are.'

'And what's that like?'

'Well, I thought – when we first met you, we thought you were, kind of like – don't take this the wrong way, will you?'

'No,' I laughed. 'I won't. Go on.'

'We thought you were, like, trouble.'

'Trouble?'

'All that stuff with Ben?'

The Cats had been there when Ben was losing it a bit, trying to pick a fight with Adam when I first met him. 'Oh, that. Old stuff. All that's over and done with.'

'Yeah, so I see. We thought, at the time, you and Ben – you know. Something happened between you? Car Crime?'

'Yeah,' I said. 'Car Crime.'

'Still,' Angel said, 'it looks like you and Adam now, doesn't it?'

'Does it?'

'Looks like it,' she said, about to laugh.

We both laughed. We got ready for bed. It was going to be an early start in the morning, so we were supposed to go to sleep straight away. This was the first time we'd shared a room. Straight to sleep? Can you, when you feel like we did, all wound up and excited? We were talking. It was dark. Angel wanted to tell me some stuff. I wanted to tell her some of mine. We exchanged stuff: details, family, school, friends, boyfriends, all that. Boyfriends again, all that. Boy-friends.

Angel told me about this boy who had gone about saying all kinds of horrible things about her. She told me he made her sound cheap and like rubbish. He told everyone about the things they'd talked about and tried out together.

'Why did he do it?' I asked.

'Why do they ever do it?' she said. 'I don't know why. What's in it for them? He only made me hate him. I thought I really, really liked him, but he made me hate him. I hated myself too, for a while.'

'I know what you mean,' I said.

'You do?'

'Yeah, I do,' I said. I told her about Jagdish.

'Jagdish Mistri?' she said. 'Asian boy?'

'Dancer. Jagdish Smith, actually. His father was from London, his mother from India.'

'Nice.'

'Yeah. Very.'

'What happened?'

So I told Angel all about it. She listened to me. She understood. We understood one another. That first night in that little hotel in Paris was like finding an old friend in a new person. We were supposed to go to sleep early, but ended up staying awake talking for hours and hours. We tried not to. Every so often, we'd at least try to doze off, until one or the other of us thought of something else we felt we just had to say. It was one of those times you just have to say it – do you recognise those times? The dark silence in the night all round us was waiting to be spoken through: those few silences between us nothing more than gaps to be filled with words.

Angel told me about her brothers. There were two of them: one nice, a quiet boy, the other a mouthy idiot, trying to get drunk at fourteen years old, or smoking weed in the park with the other idiots he hung around with. I told Angel about my sisters.

'I've seen pictures of Jo and George,' she said. 'They were in some of the mags. They look like great fun.'

'They are,' I said, suddenly missing my family, my friends. I told Angel about Leo and about Beccs. Angel said she didn't really have a best friend, not one as close as Beccs, anyway.

'I've always wanted a friend like that,' she said, across the darkness between our twin beds.

We stopped talking for a few moments. Those moments were ours, to share. They passed; we, however, did not pass over them. They stayed between us, shared. We talked about lots of other things, all of them shared across that gap between our beds, as if over the space of those few moments after Angel had admitted wanting a dear and very good friend. For a while I wondered if I was guilty of pushing Beccs out; but Beccs wouldn't mind, I knew that. She'd understand how much I needed other friends.

By the morning, with not much sleep behind us, that was what we were, Angel and I, two tired, but dear, very good friends.

# ✦✦✦ Twelve

It was impossible to work so closely without characters clashing and crashing every now and then. We each had a tantrum, every so often. When Adam wasn't around for a whole day, day and a half, I felt a lot more jumpy and unconfident. Angel sensed it. She was with me. And I was with her whenever she and the other Cats felt like scratching each other's eyes out.

Then my mum was with me, with us, amongst the creation and confusion. It was too lovely to see her; I felt quite upset for a few minutes. When I'd left home, however many days ago, I hadn't known I'd be gone for so long. It's never a good thing, going away without saying goodbye properly. Before I knew it, I was saying hello with a lump in my throat, feeling almost as if I'd done this on purpose – running away, I mean, just as things were heating up for my mum in her role as part of my management team.

She was having none of that, though. 'This is perfect,' she smiled. She was happy. I wanted to hug her. She hugged me. 'We're going to make this work,' she said.

After I introduced her to everybody, she went off to talk to Pierre, while Ben and I went through some of the old Car Crime stuff we had – or he had, to be more accurate:

*Whatever you do it's insane,*
*You can't look back.*

*Locked in the right-hand lane,*
*You're on the wrong track.*
*What have you done?*

*Wherever you're going to*
*Keep your heel to the floor.*
*It's all over now, baby, for you,*
*They can't touch you any more.*
*What have you done?*

'I haven't done a thing,' another voice said from the doorway. 'Not yet, anyway.'

We both recognised that voice; we would have known it anywhere, amongst however many others.

'Leo!' I cried out. Still almost spilling over from seeing my mum, here was Leo in Paris to see me, mincing into the room, absolutely daring me to shed a tear by the look of mock-stern seriousness on his face.

I laughed out loud, running to him. 'Oh, it's – I can't tell you –'

'Then don't, Lovely. Be happy.'

'I am happy, Leo. I am.'

'I can see. Hello, Ben. Is she being too much bother, quite?'

'Not quite,' Ben smiled. He shook hands with Leo. 'I'll leave you to – you know,' he said, making his way out.

Leo held me by the upper arms at arm's length, inspecting me. He had his soft-leather bag slung over one shoulder. 'Let me look at you. Oh, sweet, are you sleeping? You're not sleeping! Leo knows. You look lovely, but Leo knows. I can read the contours of your face, and I'm not even joking.'

'I know you're not, Leo. But what are you doing here, first? I mean, it's fantastic to see you – but Ray. What about Ray?'

He swatted the world away. 'No,' he said, 'no, you first. I'm here to see how you are – for my own sake, nobody else's. Ray doesn't know where I am. I'm not sure he cares at the moment – but he doesn't know, that's the important thing. I have to be sure my girl's all right, don't I? I told you, I'm never going away, whatever happens. Leo's always with you,' he said, as I hugged him, as he hugged me.

'Now,' he said, drawing away, 'I have something for you. To help you sleep.'

'Leo,' I said, stepping back, 'I don't want to take any –'

'Oh, Lovely,' he positively sagged, 'you think I'd – after all that's happened? Deary me, what must you think of me? Look, this is what I've brought you.' He was unwrapping some silk thing with strings, opening a box. 'Look,' he said, holding them out to me.

'What are they?'

'Have a look. Look,' he said, putting the silky thing over his eyes. It was like some kind of blank mask. 'It's an eye-patch,' he grinned under it. 'I can't see you. I can't see anything. It's fantastic!'

'Oh, you sleep with one of these on, do you?'

'I do now. It really works. You'll be surprised how quickly you get used to it. Before you know it, you can't sleep without it. And these. Look. Earplugs. Wax. You put one in each ear. Sleep? You can sleep anywhere. You can't see or hear anything.'

I laughed. 'Perfect!'

'You'll have to get a really loud alarm clock,' Leo said.

'I've got one. She's called Angel. No problem. Anyway, what's it been like, with Ray?'

Leo shrugged, trying to make light of the anxiety that had suddenly slipped into my voice. 'I've been keeping out of his way. He'll throw tantrums, he'll attack where he can. He'll consult his lawyer. But in the end, he needs you more than you need him.'

'Oh,' I almost laughed, 'I don't think Ray needs anyone really.'

'Sweet, that's one of the reasons he's so afraid of you. I told you, that's Ray's way. He needs you, you need – look at you! What do you need? Nothing. You have the talent Ray so covets – do you understand what I mean?'

There had been times, in the past, when I'd have had to answer no to that question. But now I said, 'Yes,' because I did. 'Just be careful, Leo. You're as vulnerable as I am, don't forget.'

He laughed. He sparkled. Considering everything that had happened, Leo was surprisingly carefree. 'I'm going to show him how stupid he is,' he said again. 'I'm not afraid any more.'

'I'm not afraid any more,' I said to Beccs over the phone that evening.

'When were you ever?' she said.

This was the first time in ages I'd been able to speak to her. She told me she'd been studying too hard lately, making herself too tired, sleeping badly with a head full of swirling, unwelcome middle-of-the-night thoughts. I knew what that was like, but Beccs didn't seem to want to share any of that with me. This was so unlike us.

'You'll be off to uni next year,' I said. 'And I'll be – I don't know where I'll be, or what I'll be doing. That's what's always frightened me, it's the uncertainty of everything. That's why I've always envied you so much, Beccs.'

'What, my routine life?'

'No, your certainty. You can make the things you want to happen, happen.'

'It's not as easy as that.'

'No, I know. But you know what I mean, don't you? I've never known what I'm supposed to be doing from one week to the next. At least you're working towards something.'

'So are you now.'

'Yes, I think so. It feels like it, anyway.'

'And you're working with Ben.'

'And all the others. Angel. I really want you to meet Angel. She's great. A friend, you know?'

'I know,' Beccs said. But she sounded as if she knew something else. Beccs sounded as if she knew different. After a pause, she said, 'And Adam?'

'Yes, Adam.'

Another pause went by. 'Well?' she said.

'Well what?'

She snorted out a kind of brief laugh. 'You know what! Is he going on tour with you? And if he is – is he?'

'No. I don't know.'

'No? Or you don't know?'

'I can't – it's all over the place, Beccs. He'll be with us sometimes, not others. It's weird. It's like how I feel. One moment I feel one thing, the next I – I don't change my mind, I just seem to forget what my mind was. I keep going back to feeling – you know –'

I thought she was going to say something. I waited. She didn't.

'I'm waiting for something,' I said. 'Something to happen.'

'Oh, yes?'

'No, I don't mean like that. I don't know what I mean. There's still something I've got to overcome before I can let anyone near enough to hurt me.'

'You still think he might hurt you?'

'No, I don't.'

'I don't understand.'

'Neither do I. But I'm too busy to worry about it. I'll think about it when everything else calms down.'

'If it ever does.'

'Oh, it will. One day.'

'Adam might not still be about, on that day.'

'So what should I do, Beccs? Tell me what to do and I'll do it.'

Beccs let out another little snort of non-laughter. She didn't tell me what to do. 'You'll be all right,' she said. 'You'll survive.'

I had wanted something more than that, from Beccs, more than simply survival. I'd wanted her blessing to put with the blessings I'd received that day from Leo and from my mum.

Angel laughed at me that night as I stuffed my ears full of wax plugs and masked my eyes. But Leo was right; I went off to sleep. I would survive, although I wanted to feel blessed. I tried to feel it. Tomorrow we would be at the beginning of the first day of a Car Crime tour. We were unknown. We were raw. It was complete madness. But I would survive.

Let the madness begin.

# ***⁎ Thirteen

**W**hen it goes well on stage – when hit by that extreme high that comes with a good performance and there's nothing left in the world but the way it feels to be up there – it's so difficult to come down afterwards. We were all affected. Well, eventually. The first few gigs were disastrous, after all. We were billed as 'Amy Peppercorn and Car Crime, featuring the Static Cats'. Nobody wanted it this way, least of all me, but Pierre said we had to use the name I'd already made for myself. For all our efforts, the new songs were too new, the old ones – what there were of them – too ill-prepared. It was crazy. We needed more rehearsals, but there simply wasn't time. We just had to get on with it.

In the beginning, when we messed it up, none of us had the confidence to shrug or dance it off. We stumbled time and again in front of sparse audiences, tripping over each other both physically and verbally. I had no experience of so many performers on stage all at once, what with Ben, our guitarist Dave, and the three Cats and me all crammed on some very small stages. I'd worked with backing singers, yes; but the Cats were never just this. They were all trying to be performers in their own right. Ben was getting frustrated. He was trying to hold the whole thing together, trying not to lose his temper. It didn't work.

'What did you think you were supposed to be doing?' he yelled at Kaylie first. This was after the second gig. The first had been and gone in a little club in Frankfurt, a shameful shambles from a bunch of amateurs in front of just a few tired Monday evening clubbers. Nothing worked for us. The sound system was set up all wrong for what we were trying to do. It was pathetic – we were, every one of us. Nobody said a thing afterwards. We all had to lend a hand lugging out the equipment, which we did in shameful silence. This I was not used to. It came as a kind of rude awakening for me, that things could go this wrong, and I'd have to help lift equipment in and out of dreary premises.

After the second gig, which didn't really go any better than the first, that was when Ben lost it with Kaylie. 'You were all over the place!'

'Me!' she screeched. 'Me! What about her? She was all over the place, not me!'

The 'she' she was shouting about was Miranda. Until then the two of them, Kaylie and Miranda, had been vying for Ben's attention. Now when Kaylie had it, she didn't want it.

'Don't go blaming me!' Miranda screamed back.

It is hard to come down from the high after a good performance; but it's even more difficult trying to kick the low of a bad one. The only good thing I had so far was the sleeping-kit Leo had given me. Angel was turning and turning in bed that night, switching on the light over her side of the room, reading a magazine, trying too hard to sleep. I took a peak at her every now and then from under my eye-patch. Other than that, I couldn't see or hear; I was alone at night in peace and quiet. You see, however bad it was for Ben and Dave and the Cats and the others, this, for me, was still better than the loneliness I'd suffered from for so very long. All day we were together, so come night-time, I was grateful for the eye and ear isolation Leo had granted me.

I thought about lots of things. I slept. The others had

trouble. I dreamt of the sun on my back in France, and Adam was there, in the dream, in my dreams.

Three performances later, and we were bouncing off the stage of that lively little club in Hamburg. That was where we were – Hamburg – I remember now. How could I have forgotten? We had played a couple of different places in Hamburg, but this was the first time we – as I said, when we came off after that third gig, Friday night I think, we were flying. I'd been there before of course, lots of times; in that feeling of flight, that manic, crazy rush from which height the whole world seems to be at your feet. But this time I was up there with the angels, with Angel, with Miranda and Kaylie and Ben and Dave, and we were screaming in the dressing room afterwards and bouncing off the walls.

In every performance, success depends not only upon the performer, but the audience. There is always a certain stage at which it starts to go right, when the audience starts to feel itself with you and you respond to their response.

'Did you feel it?' Angel was screaming at me. 'Did you feel it? Did you? Did you feel what I felt?'

We were all shouting at the tops of our voices.

'It was like –'

'No way! No way was I expecting that! No way! No way was I!'

'It's like –'

'Car Crime!'

'Car Crime!'

We recited 'Car Crime' like a mantra, or some kind of club catchphrase. You had to be in on it. If you were, wow! And we were!

116

'Car Crime!'

Because we'd committed ourselves on stage to the acceleration of sound as we shifted from cruise control into overdrive, screaming in excitement and near-fear as Ben's thrashing car crash beat nearly threw us into a spin at every corner. Ben did it for us. We were doing his music, more dance/urban than my pop background; but Ben was back on form, driving everything forward from the stage backseat, spurring the three Cats and me on to greater and greater breakneck speeds. I don't know how he did it, just using sound and words, but the levels of danger and excitement came up and caught us, or caught the audience first, and thrust us all forward until we were white-knuckled and hanging on for dear life.

For life was dear. All of a sudden the dear idea of Car Crime, constructed of disparate elements as it was, came together, like parts on a production line creating a whole greater than themselves. Angel and Kaylie and Miranda and Amy were like one unit, components of the same thing as the speed increased with the acceleration of our – and Ben's – performance. Ours and Ben's and Dave's and the sound man's and the driver's; we were all involved.

That Friday night, after the gig, we would have gone out to celebrate like mad with all the madness in our souls, had we not had to deconstruct the kit and get it all out and get back to the hotel for a half-decent night's sleep before an early start for another German city first thing in the morning. As it was, the hotel was no place of tranquillity or rest with all of us in it, with our energy levels up and the mania of adrenalin overdosing our brains. It eventually erupted into one massive pillow fight in Ben's room. Pillows from the other room appeared as we laid into each other. We were just so up, there was nothing else we could have done. I'd read about people in bands trashing hotel rooms – our pillow fighting was never that destructive, but now I understood how such a thing could happen. I'd known for a long time how dangerous this feeling was, but being with everyone else, knowing they all felt the same, magnified the intensity of the energy beyond any control.

Pillow fights don't usually last very long. This one did. It didn't stop until we were all just about spent and our energy lay scattered with the cushions from the room sofa, or screwed up in Ben's bed linen.

Miranda relaxed, as she thought the fight was nearly over, only to catch the last hefty pillow thump from Kaylie, thudding feathery but still hard into Miranda's face. She'd been standing on the bed at the time and went flinging back with the strength of the blow. It *was* hard, too. Kaylie had seemed to put all her strength into it, sending Miranda flying backwards off the bed to the floor, where her head met the thin covering of carpet with such a smack it set my teeth on edge.

'Oh my God!' Angel cried.

'Leave her!' Ben shouted, as the rest of us leapt forward to where she was lying.

We stopped, all of us. Miranda was very, very still, with her head to one side, her hair flung across her face. The silence was oppressive. Nobody moved. Miranda was so still, she didn't even look as though she was breathing.

Ben went to her, kneeling over her, gently pushing the hair from her face. 'Miranda,' he said. 'Miranda. Don't be hurt.'

Angel and I exchanged glances. I looked at Kaylie, whose horrified concentration was fixed firmly upon Miranda's inexpressive and apparently lifeless face.

'Miranda,' Ben said, touching her face.

Miranda's head fell back.

We thought – we all thought –

But then she was laughing. Her stomach started to do a kind of hiccough with the silent laughter she couldn't hold in any longer. Her eyes flew open, her head coming up close, so very close to Ben's. 'Give us a kiss,' she said. He didn't, but she kissed him anyway, a quick, stolen peck on the lips.

'You!' Kaylie screeched, going for her with the pillow once again. She whacked Ben one, accidentally. Or maybe it wasn't an accident.

In a moment, we were all back to thwacking each other, bouncing on the beds, screaming and laughing, still trying to burn off the excess energy of wild adrenalin pumping through us.

It didn't work.

Nobody slept very well that night. My eye-patch and earplugs were good for isolation – I could be in silence and darkness anywhere, on a midday beach if necessary – but they couldn't give my mind a rest if it didn't want to slow down. It didn't want to, that was for sure. Next morning we were up and downstairs for breakfast dead early, all looking the worse for wear, as if we'd had that night out celebrating after all. Perhaps we had, but not out. We looked like we all needed a hot bath and a good telling off before bed. There was no one to tell us off but ourselves. It was great!

We were travelling from place to place, singing in the backs of vans, fighting, playing games, trying to catch up on lost sleep: failing at that. I didn't know it could be like this.

Ben, I suppose, was like some kind of authority figure.

119

None of the few road-crew was interested in what we got up to. Our driver or Dave the guitarist couldn't have cared less. Ben had to calm us down sometimes, especially when fights, real fights, looked about to break out.

Like when I suggested we all wore pink. Pink, I'd always thought, was a soppy colour. It always had been for me, anyway. But I had this idea that if all four girls, with all our different skin colours and tones, were in pink outfits, not exactly the same outfit, but everything in a similar pink, we'd look like something; something you didn't see every day, anyway.

'Pink?' Kaylie sneered. 'Pink?'

'Pink?' Angel said.

'Yeah,' I smiled. I was getting more enthusiastic the more I thought about it. 'Pink. You know, baby pink. Then it doesn't matter – skirts, trousers, tops, bikini tops, shoes, boots, everything pink. Think about it.'

'I am!' Kaylie sneered again. 'And it's making me feel sick.'

'No,' Angel said, 'no. Think about it. It's like –'

'It's rubbish!' Kaylie said.

'No,' Miranda said now, 'I think it's good. I think it's really good. What do you think, Ben?'

Ben wasn't always with us when we were travelling. I don't think he could stand too much of it, with Kaylie and Miranda bouncing competitive comments off him all the time.

'Yeah,' said Kaylie, still with a sneer in her voice, 'what do you think, Ben?' she said, doing a whingeing impression of Miranda.

'Why don't you grow up?' Miranda said.

'Why don't you shut up?'

'Hey!' Ben yelled. He was sitting up front with the driver, turning to glare into the back at the rest of us. 'Can you lot give it a rest? What do you sound like? Do you know what you sound like? If you did, you'd be quiet back there.'

'Yeah,' said Kaylie.

'Yeah, you' – from Miranda.

'I know what you mean, Ben,' Kaylie said, ignoring Miranda.

Ben tutted and faced the front again. But we were silent for a while after that.

A few days later we sorted out or bought stuff in baby pink, just as I said, and we looked fantastic, just as I said. It was strangely weird, being the one who said what we should do. Stranger still, that Ben should be the one to bring sobriety and stability to the shambles that we could have been if not for him. When I considered the mess he'd been in just a little while ago – it was so good to see him like this. It made me want to laugh quite a bit, only I tried not to, unless it was in private with Angel.

'What are you going to do about Adam?' she asked me, in confidence.

I didn't mind telling her I didn't know. I couldn't think about it. There was too much going on, too many laughs and arguments and jealousies and sympathies. And there was never enough sleep.

Nobody asked me about my epilepsy, not once. So I didn't bother mentioning it, except to Angel of course. I took my medication every day, without fail. Angel asked me what it was I kept having to swallow twice a day, every day. She shrugged when I told her. People usually asked me what they should do if I went into a seizure; they wanted to ask what it was like to have a fit, but didn't like to ask. Angel just shrugged. She didn't ask anything. I liked that, the way she made light of the unimportant things.

***

We made light of just about everything. Nothing mattered that much. If we were having a good time, that was all there was to it.

Like this:

Being on stage in a club for a short set, which is what most of our gigs were: let's face it, we didn't exactly have masses of material. But what we did have was good, and we were growing in confidence all the time. Our stage act was really beginning to come together. The Cats and I were wearing pink in Cologne in a club not far from the square where the beautiful cathedral stands. It was a dance club primarily, and we were the sort of live band act in the interval between DJs. There was a lull in activity in the place, with hardly anybody prepared to dance as soon as the recorded sounds stopped. Some people stood and watched us, but mostly they started to disappear to the bar or to the toilet or to the tables scattered round the outsides. Anyway, we weren't exactly considered a star turn, obviously. It was a scary feeling, to think that nobody was going to take any notice of us. We were all imagining coming off stage at the end of our set to a thunderous silence that would only stop with the start of the next DJ.

But Ben set us up and got us going as usual, starting with a slow rev from his cool engines, his beat-boxes and synthesizers. He nodded and gesticulated furiously, as if he were dancing out of tune. We were dancing out of time, off tune, too intimidated to take the lead and drive this thing forward. Ben had to do it, so he did.

It reminded me of the school concert I'd done with Ben ages ago, at the beginning of Car Crime. It felt the same, with an uninterested audience not expecting much. Well, we were going to give them something more than that.

I hadn't screamed for, oh, a long time. But Ben's crime-crazy beat pumped me up for this, for my step forward up to the mike as if about to sing. I screamed. The whole place jumped. So did we – three Static Cats and me – as Ben jammed the throttle forward and we were thrust into thrash before the imminent danger of crash and peril. This was dangerous. There was excitement but also fear in it. It made us all feel like screaming.

The floor before us filled suddenly with a flood of people. I'd forgotten what it was like to scream like that; to have Ben catch hold of it and accelerate it into the distance with everybody, the Cats and the audience and me, hanging on for dear life. I'd been here before, committing car crime like this, with Ben; but nobody else had. It was new. It was dangerous, but so far nobody had been hurt. Our past felt dead and buried. The only things that counted were the scream, the speed, the furtherance of speed, the slowing down, the expected stop. We didn't stop. The girls and I were onto this. We screamed, all four of us, and the whole thing began again:

*Come with me, run with me,*
*Laugh and have fun with me,*
*Tell me now what do you say?*
*There's nowhere to hide with me,*
*Take a joy ride with me,*
*Nothing can stand in our way!*

*We're going nowhere,*
*But lookin' good while we get there.*
*So follow if you dare,*
*To destination anywhere.*

123

*We're both out on a roll, runnin' out of control,*
*Hold me, don't let me go!*

We were out on a roll, runnin' out of control. What a buzz! And we thought we'd done well on other nights! They were nothing compared with this. Because nothing compared with this – and I'd done gigs in huge halls and arenas. It was the contrast; the way everyone was so bored with us in the beginning, compared with the tumult of applause and appreciation at the end of our set. We'd been on at least three times longer than our original allocated time. We'd have liked to be on a lot longer but we ran out of material. We needed more songs.

A pillow fight wasn't nearly enough to burn us out that night. We had to stay at that club in Cologne and dance – me, Angel, Kaylie, Miranda, Ben and Dave the guitarist. We kept our pink stuff on, we four girls, so stood out as a unit on the crowded dance floor. We were so full of energy, even in the cab on the way back to the hotel there was all sorts of banter and harmless insults going round, as Kaylie and Miranda both bickered, trying to get close to Ben, and guitarist Dave had a strange and unsteady go at getting close to Angel. Kaylie cornered me however, later that night. We should have been in bed hours before. Instead:

'You've known Ben a long time, haven't you?'

'No, not that long. We were at school together, for a while. That's where Car Crime started.'

'Yeah,' she said, 'I know all that. I just, you know, wondered why Ben's not – like, as Angel reckons, as if he's still, you know – like for you and him?'

'Me and him?'

'Yeah. No?'

'No. No me and him.'

Kaylie looked reassured.

'Why, what did Angel say?'

'Oh, nothing. Just, you're not actually with Adam, as such, are you?'

'Oh. I'm – how did you – how do you know?'

'Oh. You know.'

She smiled. You know. Only I didn't know. Something about this made me feel uneasy and confused. I smiled too, saying nothing.

'So there's no reason – with Ben? Nothing to – he hasn't got a girlfriend or anything, anywhere, has he?'

'I don't know.'

'Oh. I thought you would. Only Angel said –'

'Angel said?'

'She said you were good friends, you and Ben. I wondered just how good, that's all.'

'What's she on about?' Miranda said, ambling over to where we were sitting.

'We thought you'd gone to bed,' I said.

'So I see,' she said, poking a look at Kaylie.

'What?' Kaylie said. 'What?'

'Ben, is it?' Miranda asked me.

'No,' Kaylie said, quickly, 'it's Adam, actually. So that shows how much you know, doesn't it? Nothing. That's all you know.'

'I know more than you do.'

'You don't! She doesn't!' she said to me.

Who said to me? By this point in all of their bickering rows I could never remember for a single second who had said what, about what, or why. It always degenerated into picky little personal insults thrown between the two of them, each asking for back-up from the third party involved, whoever it happened to be at the time. I was forever trying to ensure it wasn't me. This time it was.

'Anyway,' Miranda said to Kaylie, 'you should mind your own business about Adam, shouldn't she, Amy?'

'I don't –'

'Oh,' I said. 'Just leave me out of it, will you? And Adam.' I gave up on them and went to bed. Angel was still up, doing her face. 'Don't those two drive you mad?' I said.

She stiffened. She knew exactly who I was talking about. 'What they been saying now? Don't you take any notice,' she said, without waiting for an answer to her question. 'You know what they're like. They run round and round in circles, squawking.'

I laughed. 'A couple of birds. Exactly.'

'Both pecking up crumbs. Boy-crumbs.'

'Ben-crumbs,' I laughed.

'Yeah,' she laughed too. 'If only they knew.'

'Knew? Knew what?'

Angel glanced at me in the mirror. 'How much Ben likes me,' she said, glancing at me again.

'Does he?' I said, surprised.

'Yes. Haven't you noticed? You can't say you haven't noticed!'

'Well, I told you, I know he likes you.'

'He does,' she said, sounding satisfied, 'he likes me a lot.'

'What, has he said so?'

'Oh, yeah. All the time.'

All the time? I'd never noticed.

'But I'm like you,' Angel said. She turned from the dressing-table mirror to face me. 'You know, that's what gets them. That's what makes them interested, when you don't care. If I

126

was forever running after Ben like those two birds, do you think he'd be interested?'

'No,' I said. 'Probably not.'

'No. Course not. That's what does it. You'll see. As soon as you give Adam the go-ahead, he'll lose interest, believe me. As soon as you –'

But there was a smash against our bedroom door, a scream, a thump. We jumped up. I flung open the door and Kaylie and Miranda tumbled in and fell on the carpet in a tussle of loose hair and limbs.

'You lying cow!'

'You're the cow, cow!'

'Cow!'

'Cow!'

Angel and I stood watching them wrestling on the floor, unsure for a moment whether or not they were joking. Then Miranda pulled Kaylie's hair with such force, producing a scream so loud, neither we nor just about anybody else in that little boarding house was left unsure of how serious a fight this was becoming.

But before we could make a move to separate them, Ben was in the room, followed closely by Dave, each picking up a girl from the floor, holding the two spitting, scratching Cats well away from each other. 'What's happening?' Ben said.

'That cow!'

'No! You! Cow!'

'No! You!'

'Angel?' Ben said. He seemed to be asking her something with his eyes. The gesture didn't go unnoticed by anyone, including the warring factions being held back by their arms. They went from staring at each other to looking at Angel.

Ben seemed to be waiting for Angel to do something to sort this out, as if he expected her to be their leader. But the other two clawing Cats were turning the spite of their slit-eyed attention towards her.

'Look,' I said, stepping forward, 'let's just keep our fights to using pillows, shall we?'

There seemed to be something going on, some kind of struggle for strength and power beyond the scratch and scramble of the tangle of fighting limbs and furious hair. Angel and Ben certainly did seem to have some kind of mutual understanding, I could see. So could Kaylie and Miranda, as they dragged free of their captors, both grabbing pillows and laying into Angel and into Ben and Dave and me. Mostly into Angel, though.

This was getting too crazy. We were supposed to be on the road again in a few hours or so, and here we were all laying into each other until somebody else complained about us and the hotel manager was called out of bed to deal with us and we were all sent to our own beds thoroughly ticked-off and invited never to return to his hotel again, ever. Any of us.

# ✦✦✦ Fourteen

I wrote a song. I'd written the lyrics to *Destination Anywhere*; but somehow, sitting in the back of a van trundling along an autobahn, I managed to compose a song, complete: lyrics, tune, everything. The strangest thing was, I'd never, ever had an original tune in my head before. There seemed to be something about the motion of the van, the rhythmic sense of time passing, punctuated by pepperings of odd conversations, statements of hunger, thirst, jokes, laughter, groans, sighs, arguments. Always arguments.

'What's it called?' Ben said.

I sang it to him. It was called *Living the Dream*. It said something about what I'd been through, where I was now and where I was going. The song seemed to mean so much to me, much more than I'd realised as I was writing it.

Ben could see, I was sure, what was going on inside me as I sang. 'Who wrote the tune?' he asked, as soon as I stopped. 'You did? You did everything?'

'What do you think?'

'What do I think? What do I think?'

The very next night, Car Crime performed the new song on stage. Ben had shown me exactly what he had thought of my song by arranging it so quickly, doing a great job with it. He made it sound like – like a proper song composed by a proper songwriter, not just little me in the back of a van with an earful of squawks and squabbles. I texted Beccs, to let her know just how good Ben was. I sent her the whole of the lyrics. It was the longest text I'd ever sent. 'Sounds Good!' she sent me back.

Angel and I sang most of it together, with Kaylie and Miranda coming in on backing and chorus. This was my new song. *Living the Dream*. I did it. We performed it:

*So let me down again*
*Why don't you?*
*I thought you were a friend*
*Why weren't you?*

*I needed you*
*You weren't there.*
*So let me down again*
*See if I care.*

*You never knew me through and through*
*There was always a part of me*
*That lived at the heart of me*
*That was never, ever you.*

My song. My words, my melody. If it sounded pessimistic, if it made me sound as if I'd been damaged, I hadn't, because it went on like this:

*I'm living it such a lot*
*I'm giving it all I got*
*I'm living my dream.*
*If you think I've lost*
*I've not.*
*I can't be double-crossed*
*I'm hot.*

*I'm not what I seem*
*I'm giving it one last shot*
*One final scream.*
*I'm living the dream!*

Oh, and I was living it, believe you me. I was hot, giving it all I got. To hell with good or bad grammar – giving all I got, one final scream, living the dream.

Oh yes, and what made it all so much better was when I noticed Adam, standing there to one side smiling, with Pierre, unexpected; a super-charged flush of unanticipated excitement and pleasure.

*So come round here and see*

I sang.

*There's nothing I can't do.*
*Who needs an enemy*
*With friends like you?*

I looked away from Adam as I sang that, finding myself eye to eye with Angel. She seemed to have been concentrating on Adam, or Pierre. Or Adam.

Adam was looking at me as I sang:

*All I need is me*
*And there's nothing you can do.*

*You never knew me through and through*
*There was always a part of me*
*That lived at the heart of me*
*That was never, ever you.*

We were looking at each other. It was better than I'd imagined, seeing Adam again. He looked so, just so – you know!

*I'm living it such a lot*
*I'm giving it all I got*
*I'm living my dream.*
*If you think I've lost*
*I've not.*
*I can't be double-crossed*
*I'm hot.*
*I'm not what I seem*
*I'm giving it one last shot*
*One final scream.*
*I'm living the dream!*

And he looked like a dream, standing there next to Pierre. I seemed to have forgotten quite what he looked like. Now I remembered; boy, did I remember!

The rest of the show flew by so fast and so furiously, I had trouble remembering any of it. All I know is that I was performing for Adam, showing him what I could do, what I'd done with Ben and the Cats to turn Car Crime into a working band. Of course I was showing Pierre Piatta too; wanting to demonstrate how his trust and faith in me hadn't been misplaced. I wanted Pierre to see this is what I was, this singer/songwriter up there performing her own material, with a good team around her. This was exactly what I wanted now, to be this, not that lost and lonely Solar starlet pushed from pillar to post and back again.

It worked, too. From where I stood singing, as I moved, as we danced, as we committed ourselves to the performance, the effect on Pierre was obvious. He liked what he heard and saw.

So did Adam. 'You were good!' he cried, reaching to embrace me as I approached in pink: pink, but with a dazzle of blue lapis lazuli at my throat.

'Did you really like it? What are you doing here? I wasn't expecting to – did you really like it?'

He laughed. 'Oh, yes,' he said. He kissed me, lightly, but tenderly. 'I liked it very much. We have come as a surprise. We have – Pierre has something to say – to you all.' He touched the bright pendant.

'I haven't taken it off,' I said.

'Not at all?'

'Not at all,' I said, feeling quite flushed, slightly dizzy and light-headed. Adam made me feel like this, making me feel as if I wanted to make him feel like kissing me properly. I'd forgotten, somehow, what this was like.

'She's here, Pierre,' Angel was saying, leading Pierre to the little dark recess where Adam and I had manoeuvred each other in our effort to make that proper kiss. 'She's here. Oh, hello Adam.'

Adam didn't say anything.

'Amy!' Pierre sang out, coming to kiss me on both cheeks. 'You have been producing songs, I hear? You are beginning to bloom?'

I had to smile. From the corner of my eye I caught the smile Adam was giving me, as Angel watched him fiercely.

'Yes,' Pierre said. 'But now I have something to tell you.'

'Oh yes?'

'Yes. I have to tell you this: the tour is now at an end.'

# ✷✷✷ Fifteen

**S**o, abruptly, it was over. My heart sank. We were all to travel back to Paris early next morning. All of our other German and French venues had been put on hold.

I asked Pierre what was going on. He wouldn't say exactly, revealing only that there would be an important meeting between PPF, Solar Records and me.

'Solar Records?' I asked in alarm, picturing Ray Ray's dipped face glowering like an angry sunset at one end of the table, with me at the other, shrivelling.

Pierre had nodded, mysteriously. He looked serious. The whole situation, everything I was doing, felt about to change again. And I didn't want it to. 'Ah, but you are not to worry,' Pierre smiled. 'We shall see. We shall see.'

'So,' Angel was sitting up in bed asking, 'what did he say? What did he say? I'm dying to know.'

'Say? He didn't say anything,' I said. Pierre had told me not to worry, then he had left me alone with Adam for a while, to talk. But we hadn't done much talking. We only had ten minutes or so, or that was all it felt to me.

'But you've been ages!' Angel whined. 'Pierre must have said something? Why aren't you going to tell me?'

'There's nothing to tell.'

'Oh,' she said, collapsing onto one elbow, 'it's like that, is it?'

'Like what?'

'Like, you know. Anyway, do you trust him, Adam? I suppose you do, now.'

'Why?'

'I don't know why. You and him, off together like that. Secrets.'

'There are no secrets! Angel, look –'

'No, it's okay. I get it. Don't worry.'

'I'm not worried. Well, I am, but not in the way you mean.'

'No,' she said, 'but it's not a bad thing, a bit of worry. I'd be a bit worried, if I were you.'

'Would you? What have I got to worry about then, in your opinion?'

'Nothing, probably. I don't know. Nothing.'

'Nothing? That's all right then. Nothing. That's easy to worry about. I'm used to worrying about nothing. I do it all the time.'

She gave out a little laugh. 'Yeah, and me. It isn't worth it, is it?'

'No,' I said, going into our little shower room to clean my teeth. 'It isn't worth it,' I said to myself in the mirror above the sink.

'What?' Angel called out. 'Did you say something?'

'No! Talking to myself.'

'You want to watch that, girl. You'll find yourself disagreeing with yourself soon, then you'll start to believe there's more than one of you in there.'

I watched myself cleaning my teeth as if I was watching someone else. What Angel said had been a joke, but, like lots of jokes, it was fraught with truth. I knew what it was like, that kind of inner conflict that made you feel like more than a single person, like a thing at odds with itself.

I wiped my face with simple cleansing cream. Without my make-up my eyes looked smaller, my cheekbones less pronounced. With no platforms or high heels on I was much shorter than most people expect me to be, especially when they had only seen me on stage or on TV. Standing in the cold light of the bathroom I looked like any English girl from the suburbs. People often remarked on how pretty I was, but they weren't with me in the bathroom mirror, looking nothing like a star, nothing like my stage-self.

Angel was closer to being right than she imagined; there was more than one person in here. One of them wore make-up and pink or red-and-white clothes on stage, perched on huge heels singing her big heart out and lovin' and livin' it; the other padded around on flat feet in the bathroom, peering out through piggy eyes at the ordinary doubt reflected in the mirror. The trouble was, as far as Adam was concerned, I knew which of the two he'd recognise. The one he wouldn't have seen, the ordinary, doubting one, would soon turn him around, looking for something more suitable and better able to live up to the image of his lifestyle.

'It makes you wonder,' Angel said, as soon as I appeared at the bathroom door with the extractor fan still whirring behind me. 'Doesn't it make you wonder?'

'What? Doesn't what make you wonder?'

'You know,' she said, 'what they see, when they look at you.'

She said this, looking up at me from her bed, because she knew exactly what I'd been doing in the bathroom, looking at myself, wondering, seeing, and wondering some more.

'Shall I turn out the light?' I said, getting into bed.

'You tired?'

'I don't know. Probably not. We will be in the morning, though.'

'Oh, the morning! We're always tired in the morning. Who cares? We'll be travelling to Paris. No gig. No problem. I want to talk. I like it when we talk, don't you?'

'Yes. I do. What shall we talk about?'

'Ben. Let's talk about when you and Ben were at –'

'No. Let's talk about something else. Let's talk about you and Kaylie and Miranda. You were at school together?'

'Yeah. Not together though, really. They were in the year below me. I left before they did. I didn't see them for years. Then I met up with Miranda again and she told me about Kaylie and this other girl having a fight and breaking up the Static Cats. Miranda told me about that and about having a chance to go to Solar Records.'

'Oh. So the Cats haven't been together very long at all, then?'

'Not with us three. The others, yeah. I had to come in and get up to speed very quickly.'

'Well, you did that all right.'

'Yeah, despite all the fighting. We're always fighting.'

'I see the fighting. Miranda and Kaylie. You and them. There's always something.'

'Yeah, tell me about it. Always. Listen. Who do you – do you trust anyone?'

'Trust?'

'Listen, Amy. Watch out.'

I was waiting for something more. Nothing came. 'Watch out for what?'

She shrugged. 'I don't know. Things. Different things. If only we had more eyes, some other way of seeing more, we'd be better at judging, that's all I'm saying.'

'Seeing more?' I said. 'Like what?'

137

'Things. Stuff. Stuff you haven't seen – I don't think you have – look, next time, have a look at her earrings.'

'Earrings? Whose earrings?'

'Hers. Miranda's. Listen, it's probably nothing, but when Adam's there, so are the earrings. When he's not, neither are they, usually. There. I've said it.'

'Angel, is this really – I'm not sure I like what you're trying to say to me.'

'Amy, I'm not trying to say anything. You can't start blaming me for things, I'm not to –'

'You're the one telling tales! Why?'

'I'm your friend!'

'Aren't you Miranda's friend, then?'

'I don't want anything bad to happen. I don't think it has to. That's all. But you can take it like that if you want. I wish I'd never said anything. I really do!'

'So do I!' I snapped.

'Don't worry,' she said, turning away, throwing herself back on her bed, 'I won't in future!'

I watched her pulling up the quilt to cover herself as much as possible. We went quiet. I waited, trying to think. 'Okay,' I said at last, 'I suppose you know Miranda a lot better than I do.'

'And you know Adam better than me,' she said, looking back over her shoulder, 'so maybe I should just keep out of it. I'll just keep my big fat mouth shut!'

'No, Angel, don't be like that. I didn't mean – I shouldn't have reacted in that way. Sorry. It's just – I don't quite understand. What is it about the earrings? What's there to watch out for? Tell me, please.'

'There's nothing to tell,' she said, sitting up again. 'It's nothing, probably. It's just – you know, I can't believe you haven't noticed. Whenever Adam's around, so are the earrings.'

'Are they? What does it mean? I don't get it. Tell me – what's so special about these earrings?'

'Look,' she said, 'forget it for tonight. See what happens in the morning. Adam's travelling with us tomorrow, isn't he?'

'Yes, and Pierre.'

'All the way to Paris. Have a look for yourself. Let's get some sleep, shall we? It's going to be a long day tomorrow. For you, especially.'

'Especially for me?' I said, getting into bed.

'Your meeting, tomorrow evening?'

'Oh, yes. My meeting.'

'We'll find out then,' Angel said, snuggling back into her quilt. 'We'll find out everything tomorrow, won't we?'

Yes, Miranda was wearing them. I had never seen them before – not to my knowledge, anyway. Angel said she'd seen them; and she must have, simply because she knew about them. How I could have missed them, I do not know. They were so bright. They were so obviously, achingly blue.

They were lapis lazuli.

There are other blue stones, I had found out since Adam had given me my necklace, but not with such a hue, with such a depth of blue like – like this, this stone hanging on a gold thread at my throat, or those two miniature versions of the same thing in Miranda's ears. There was no mistaking it: lapis lazuli. A perfect match for my necklace.

First thing in the morning, with Angel looking over at me with a dreadfully pitying look; while Adam smiled at Miranda, then at me as I came over, without a break in his expression as his dark, secretive eyes shifted from blue earrings to blue necklace without a hint of a blink. Miranda

139

moved away as I came close, with not so much as a word or a nod of acknowledgement towards me. She seemed to evaporate under the heat of Adam's full smile.

All day I saw that smile. It came and went on Adam's face, but never once left my memory or my imagination. I didn't know what to make of a smile, with the blueness of those earrings flickering in and out of my cornered eyesight on the coach through three European countries on our way back to Paris. I wanted to ask Adam about lapis lazuli, but Angel's pitying face warned me off. She, more than anyone, recognised in the brilliance of a smile the more than coincidence in earrings and necklace hanging separately on Miranda, on me. 'If you ask about these kinds of things,' Angel said, 'people deny it. What else could they do? People lie.'

But I still wanted to ask Adam for some kind of explanation. I wanted to talk to him, but not in a coach-load of people, with Miranda able to watch us, with Angel there examining and scrutinizing my every emotion. I had to hold it all in, keeping everything together until I could trust – trust? Who could I trust? Myself? Yes, myself. I had to hold on until I could trust myself to see without anger through to the truth.

Beccs' mobile always seemed to be switched off. I wanted the intimacy of speaking to her in her room, rather than on her mum's land line, but one message after another went nowhere. Then when I did get through, there was something different about her. I was trying to tell her of my doubts about Adam, about the blue earrings and everything else. She had listened to me; but her response wasn't anything like what I would have expected. All she did was ask me what I intended to do. But that was the point in calling her, I wanted to tell her – that was what she was for!

That was when I had to pull myself up, as I discovered myself giving Beccs and our friendship a purpose. Sometimes my thinking makes me seem so selfish, even to myself. Every now and then I have to take myself to one side and explain to me that I'm not the centre of the universe, however much it sometimes feels like I am.

Beccs, I felt, was thinking the same thing about me. There was a distance between us I didn't like, however much I deserved it. So when I halted to tell myself off, asking Beccs about her, about her studies, school, her life, she was guarded and off-hand, as if she couldn't be bothered to talk to me any longer than she had to. Which was confirmed to me when she ended my call as quickly as possible on some pretext or the other, something about somebody being there to see her, so she had to go and she'd speak to me again soon. It was most unlike her. It sounded as if she was talking to somebody she didn't know very well.

By the time the meeting was due to start at PPF that evening, my head was whirling with possibilities and expectations. But nothing fitted. And now I was on my way up to the offices for some kind of decision on my future involving Solar records and PPF and I didn't know whatever other organisations or individuals interested in getting a piece of me. It made me feel sick.

Lapis lazuli!

The thing was very nearly torn from my neck. My fist was round the stone ready to break the chain and have done with it, when his voice came calling from behind me on the stairs.

'Amy,' Adam's voice said.

I turned. The blue stone was still clasped firmly in a threatening fist. 'Adam. Are you coming to the meeting?'

'So I have found out. I did not know. Let's go in together, shall we?'

'No.'

'No?'

'Not yet. Wait. I want – I need to talk to you. Look,' I said, as we passed an empty office, 'let's go in here.'

Adam followed me in with a quizzical look on his face. 'Amy, are you – well?'

'I'm well. I want to talk.'

'We don't have long.'

'I don't need long.'

'Why didn't we speak today? You were not with me, all day. Why not?'

'I was thinking.'

'Yes, I know. I could see. You were thinking. What about, for so long?'

'I was thinking about you. And some of the things you've said to me. Beautiful things.'

He nodded, looking at me intently.

'You like things to be beautiful. You look for these things. And you find them, Adam, don't you?'

'I don't – understand,' he said.

I waited. Nothing happened. I sighed, breathing deeply. 'Okay. Okay. If I asked you something, would you lie to me?'

'Lie to you? Why would I?'

'Don't answer with another question. Would you lie to me?'

'No! Lie to you? No! I would not lie.'

His eyes, as I looked into them, looked like, very like the truth.

142

'But I must ask,' he said, 'why do you question me?'

'Because I'm afraid.'

'You're afraid? Of me?'

'Yes.'

'Of me?' he asked again.

I simply nodded. His reaction made me want to cry.

'Amy, you must not be afraid of me. I will not have that. Do you understand? I will not let that happen. I am the one person, the one person you should never, never be afraid of!'

'Oh – oh!' I cried, going to him. 'Oh, I'm so – wrong. I'm always so wrong – I'm confused. I'm tired, I think. We all are. We've been doing so much.'

'You haven't enjoyed it?'

'I'm not saying that. No. We've had a great time. We didn't want it to end. Then it ended so suddenly. I'm tired now it's all over. Angel and the others are. We're a little bit mad, I think.'

'Yes, I think so too,' he said, producing one of those broad but somehow serious smiles. 'But a little bit mad is good, sometimes.'

'Is it?'

'No. It is good all times. Let us be a little bit mad together. Can we?'

I smiled, with something like relief softening me. 'Why have I been so – I don't know. I'm not even sure about – about anything. Why was I so worried? I'm so stupid!'

'No, you are not stupid. Silly, sometimes, yes. Stupid, no.'

'Okay,' I smiled. 'I'm silly. But sometimes I do think I'm going a bit mad.'

'Oh, that little bit mad. It's good, don't forget. A little bit mad I like. It is very beautiful.'

'Oh, there you go!'

'Yes, here I go. How can being sane always ever be

beautiful? Mad is unusual. Beautiful is not usual. It is very unusual too. Beautiful is a little bit mad, always.'

Now he made me laugh. 'How can you be so serious and still make me laugh so much?'

'I think perhaps you are laughing at me?'

'Oh, no. No, really.'

'You are not laughing at me?'

'No. I wouldn't do that.'

'Nor I at you. Amy, we are both a little bit crazy. Why don't we put it all together to make a lot? Let's be a lot crazy, together. Why not?'

'I can't think of any reason why not,' I said.

'No,' he said, 'neither can I.'

Talking to Adam had helped me feel a lot better about having to face Ray Ray that evening. And I felt better still when I found out Ray wasn't even there. All of a sudden it wasn't Ray at all, but my mum and Leo. What a contrast!

It felt as if I hadn't seen my mum in ages. So long, in fact, as she hugged me, I think she thought I felt different, changed in some way. 'There you are!' she said, looking into my face.

'I didn't know it was going to be you here,' I said, smiling all over the face she was so closely inspecting. 'I thought – Mum, I'm so glad it's you. And you, Leo. Leo, come here. I thought Ray might have – I don't know. I didn't dare think about it.'

'My sweet,' Leo said, 'you don't need to worry about Leo and that megalomaniac. Ooh, you've lost weight. How dare you! No Raymond Raymond? I just flex my muscles in front of him like a little bantam, and that's it. Then your mum comes in and pulverises him.'

We all laughed. Leo said hello to Adam while my mum looked at me again. 'You have lost some weight,' she said.

'Have I? I didn't mean to. I suppose, what with travelling about and everything.'

'You look – nice,' my mum said, by which I could see she meant different. She was detecting a change in me. 'You look,' she said, quietly, with some regret, 'grown up.'

I hugged her again. I was going to ask if she'd seen anything of Beccs or her mum, but Pierre came in and sat us all down around the table as if we were having a proper meeting, like businesspeople. My mum looked the part, at least. Pierre looked like a sleepy Native American Indian with his shoulder-length black hair. Leo's immaculately tended locks and sparkly jumper made him look like an expensive hairdresser from an old movie. Adam looked every centimetre the pop or rock star. And I looked thinner and more grown up.

'First of all,' Pierre said, looking round at everyone in turn, 'we must let Amy know how the ending of her tour of Germany is not to be worried about. What you were doing, Amy, you and all the others, was good. Very good reports. But all this while, we have been in negotiation, have we not, Leo?'

Lovely Leo inclined his head.

'And so,' Pierre went on, 'Leo, I think, has some more to tell you now. Leo?'

Leo smiled at everyone. He looked lovely. 'Sweet,' he said, 'you've won.' He stopped.

I glanced at my mum.

'That's it,' Leo said. 'You've won. Ray didn't think you'd have the nerve. You've called his bluff. You've won.'

'But,' I said, 'what does it mean? I don't want to go back to Solar –'

'You're not going back,' my mum said. 'When Leo says you've won, he means it. You're going to work how you want to work.'

'I'm not going into Solar, ever.'

'You don't have to,' my mum said.

'You can work at PPF,' Pierre said. 'Here, or in London. We have many studio facilities available.'

'Leo will go to Solar for you,' my mum said.

'For my sins,' he smiled.

'And so will I. We'll be your artistic and business representatives.'

'But this means,' I said, faltering, not knowing whether to laugh or cry, 'this means I – this means – I don't know what it means. What does it all mean?'

'Pierre?' Adam cut in, silent until now. 'Can I tell Amy? Can I tell her?'

Pierre nodded.

Adam smiled as he looked at me. 'This, is what it means, Amy,' he began.

The Cats didn't get it at first. Neither did Ben and Dave. I let them stew for a while.

'So why was our tour stopped?' asked Angel.

The others nodded. They all wanted to know.

'Good news for you, then,' Miranda said.

'No, not just for me. Not just – listen, we can – this means we can go anywhere.'

'Anywhere?' said Angel, looking quite un-angelic.

I was nodding like crazy. 'This means – shall I tell you what this means?'

They were all staring at me: Angel, Kaylie, Miranda, Ben, Dave. All.

'This means – are you ready? Get ready. America!'

Nothing happened.

Somebody blinked.

'America!' I bellowed into their staring faces. 'Car Crime! America!'

The girls screamed. Ben turned in a circle, clapping his hands, hi-fiving with Dave. The Cats were jumping up and down as if they'd just won a fortune on the lottery. Ben, his clapping circle and hi-fiving done, seemed to brace himself. 'Car Crime?' he said.

I nodded wildly. 'Car Crime, Static Cats, Amy Peppercorn! A whole concert, a show, with just us in it. We don't need anybody else. We do the whole thing. Just us.'

The girls were like wild cats. I was with them, starry-eyed and screaming, living the dream, at least for a while.

Ben had fallen silent, stepping away, looking the other way, away from our crazed revelries into a far, far corner. The Cats were cradled into their congratulations, too enraptured by celebration to notice me breaking away. They didn't notice as I went to Ben, whom they hadn't noticed as he'd wandered off, looking into that corner but searching far from here for the way he felt.

'Ben?'

He turned. A token smile touched the corners of his mouth.

'Ben? We've done it!'

He nodded, looking away. Far away. 'It's –' he said, breathing in deeply round the single word. He stopped.

'It's everything we wanted,' I said, 'right from the beginning. Remember that? Remember that hum of excitement we'd hear, just listening to the sound equipment? This is what it meant, Ben. This is where we were going.'

'It's too good,' he said.

'No it's not, Ben.'

'I don't deserve this.'

The Cats had silenced behind me. I glanced back at them. 'Ben, you're part of this. A big part,' I said, going to him, to kiss him. The Cats all watched me. 'Isn't that right, girls?' I turned and said. 'Ben deserves this,' I said. 'All of this. Isn't that right?'

They came and gathered about him like a flock – if you can get a flock of cats, then this was one. For a moment I had caught sight of the issues of fear and guilt that still burned in Ben; but now I could shower him in Cats – if you can get a shower of cats? Whatever, Ben was placated. A rosy kind of glow came to his cheeks as he looked at me. He was pleased. He was proud.

So was I, pleased and proud to have helped bring Ben to this, his new life. He was going to be a huge success, and not just because of me. So were the Static Cats.

# **✳✳✳ Sixteen**

'**S**o are you,' Adam said to me. 'You are going to be an even bigger success than you are already.'

He and I were going to do a recording of *Never Let You Go* for the European album. In the event, that was the only addition PPF wanted to the British release.

I thought about what Adam said for a moment. 'Successful or not,' I said, 'it'll be on my own terms.'

'It's important,' Adam said.

'Yes, it is. It is important. I feel – very happy. Adam, I do feel happy. Thank you.'

'Me? Why me?'

'It's so much to do with – you've been a part of what's happened. I feel as if a great weight's been lifted off me. And I feel as if you've helped lift it.'

'If I have, I'm glad. But you are going to America, when I am not going to America. You are going away again.'

'It always seems to be the way. That's what our lives are like, Adam. We wouldn't want to change that if we could would we?'

He shrugged. 'Maybe. I don't know. At least then we could be – we could be something together.'

'But we are something together. Look what it's like when we sing. We're good together.'

'Yes, we are good together.'

'So let's be together.'

'Let's. Yes.'

So we did what we were still together in Paris to do, when everyone else had gone home, we sang:

*I think I see you everywhere,*
*Same face, same smile,*
*Same eyes, same hair,*
*Exactly as you were before.*
*We're not together any more.*

Except that we were together. Just the two of us left here, singing. But not in the studio. That was all done. I was going home in the morning for the weekend.

Following that, America.

But for now:

*How can I forget you*
*When you've never gone away from me?*
*As I go on I cannot let you*
*Age a day from me –*
*The song of your voice, your breath in my hair,*
*Your face in the new sunlight,*
*My clothes, without yours, thrown over the chair –*
*I reach for you in the night –*

'I reach for you in the night,' Adam said, softly. We'd sung this song so often together by now, but never like this. We stopped. I can't tell you how I felt. You'll have to imagine it. Put yourself in my place. Imagine that you've been through all I've been through: the doubts, the anguish, the hurt. Maybe you have. If you have, you'll know. And maybe you'll know how it felt to be here with Adam, now that I had made up my mind about him.

150

*I saw you yesterday, today,*
*I'll see you tomorrow,*
*You aren't there,*
*But I won't let you go.*
*Just cannot let you go.*

'Tomorrow you will not be here,' Adam whispered. 'But I won't let you go.'

'Don't let me go,' I breathed. 'Not now.'

'Just cannot let you go.'

'No, just cannot let you go.'

'Ames!' my dad bellowed.

'Ames!' squealed the twins. They were both wearing baseball caps, with little ponytails peeping out at the back.

My dad came tearing over to hug me, followed very closely by Jo and George. All three of them were spattered in paint. When my dad had cuddled me home and the twins had finished climbing up me, I was about as painted as they were.

'We're decorating,' my dad said, quite unnecessarily. There were dustsheets and pots of paint all over the place. 'It's only emulsion,' he said, when he saw me looking at paint in the twins' tiny ponytails, 'it'll wash out in the bath.'

'I'll have to go and take a bath now,' I said.

'No, tell us all about Germany.'

'Tell us about Germany,' Georgie said, looking up at me.

It was kind of shocking to hear my little baby sister suddenly piece together a complete sentence like that.

'Amy Peppercorn's come home,' the other twin, Jo, said, making me laugh out loud.

'It's really great to see you two,' I said, scooping them both up into my arms again. 'There's always paint being splashed about all over this house,' I said to my dad.

'We like decorating, don't we, girls?' he shrugged, grinning.

'We like decorating,' Jo and George chanted in their paint bespattered dungarees.

'Do you know what?' I said to them. 'You're my best sisters, do you know that?'

'They know that,' my dad said. 'Tell us about Paris. Tell us everything.'

'Tell us everything,' the painted girls said.

'I do need a bath, Dad. I'll tell you afterwards. Where's Mum?'

'She'll be back in an hour or so.'

'Okay. Let me have a bath. I need to call Beccs.'

'Oh, yeah,' he said. 'She called. She's going to be out. Away with her mum, somewhere. Call her on her mobile,' she said.

I couldn't believe I'd left it until I was at home to tell Beccs I was coming home. It was the excitement, and being alone in Paris with Adam – the time just went. Beccs would understand, once I'd told her everything. And I'd be telling her absolutely everything! 'I can't wait to see you,' I said, when I got through to her mobile.

'I want to see you, too,' she said, but sounding flat and uninvolved. 'I wish you'd told me you were coming, that's all.'

'Are you okay, Beccs? I'm just home for this weekend. I was hoping we could –'

'We're away, till next week.'

'Oh. Where?'

'Me and Mum are in a health spa for the next three days. You know, steam baths, massages, mineral water. Mum thinks it'll do me good.'

'Yes, I'm sure it will.'

'Amy, my battery's nearly gone. You're not supposed to have mobile phones switched on in here. It's against the –'

And gone! Against the rules, I supposed she was about to say. I had to say it for her, in my head. What a pity. I had so wanted to tell her, to tell her everything. Beccs was supposed to know, to be in on all that happened to me: last night, in Paris, I had decided to trust Adam. I wanted Beccs to know. When we sang together, Adam and I, when we didn't, when we looked at each other, when we didn't, there was too much feeling for me to deny. To deny it would have been to waste too much of myself. I had learned how not to give, until I chose to, at which time I had learned how to take simultaneously. It had begun to feel as if I was in love, if love was that feeling of wanting to give, wanting to take, to grasp, to hold and to have. That was what I wanted to tell Beccs, that Adam was different. But couldn't, because so was Beccs.

I'd tried to tell Angel, in the way I would have told Beccs. Adam was different. There was nothing I could compare him with. I'd tried, if not to make him go away, then to give him the chance to run for it. He hadn't. Adam kept coming back. Angel had suggested it was because he and I were both with PPF now. That wasn't it. Angel couldn't have understood what it was like when Adam said things were beautiful. He made them beautiful. He said I was beautiful. He made me feel it.

This was what I wanted to share with Beccs, how beautiful it was. She would have understood. She'd understand, when her batteries were recharged, when she could share my life and I hers. You know how important it was to me. Something

153

had happened to me in Paris, something important. Beccs was supposed to have been there to help me with it. If I'd listened to Angel, she would have tried to convince me I'd done the wrong thing. It didn't feel wrong. Beccs – I needed her to confirm for me that if it didn't feel wrong, it was right. I needed Beccs.

I needed my mum, too. Not that I could tell her what it was like, being with Adam in Paris, last night. I couldn't have told her that. But then, I didn't have to.

'The bad news is,' she said, when she came home, when she'd done with looking at me, looking intently over a cup of steaming tea, 'that someone from Solar will have to go to America with you.'

She waited, to gauge my reaction. 'And the good news?' I said.

'The good news is,' she smiled, 'that it's Leo.'

'Mum! That's not good news. That's great news! Leo's coming to America!'

'Yes. So you'll be properly looked after. I'll be here, dealing with Ray, as usual.'

'How is he – Ray?'

She thought about it. Quite strange, I thought, that she had to think about it. 'He's an unstable man. Deeply flawed, I think.'

'Oh, I think something similar,' I nodded, ironically.

We started to laugh. 'He'll be all right,' my mum said, 'when he gets used to the idea that he's not actually running your life any more.'

'Will he get used to it?'

'No, I don't think so. But he'll have to learn to live with it.

He is learning, I think, in his own way. Poor Leo's glad to be getting away for a while, that's for sure.'

'Yes,' I said, 'I can imagine.' Leo would be flapping and fluttering with excitement at the prospect of his first visit to the States.

'He's happy, anyway,' my mum said.

'I'm sure he is,' I said.

'I'm sure you are,' she said.

'Yes, I am. Of course I am. It's all going so well.'

'Yes, isn't it. How did it go with Adam, in Paris?'

I must have looked quite taken aback for a moment.

'The recording?' she said, giving me a particularly scrutinising look. '*Never Let You Go*?'

'Oh, yes. Good. Really good.'

'Really good?'

'Yes.'

'Adam's not going to America, is he?'

'No, he can't. He has other engagements.'

'Mm. It works well between you, doesn't it, that song?'

'Yes, it does.'

'Yes,' she said, still scrutinising me. 'It works well between you.' She was saying this not as if she was speaking to me, but to herself. A thought seemed to pass through her mind. She was looking at me, looking at me so carefully I had to get up and move about, or else she'd have seen right inside me. I stood by the sink.

My mum sat at the table finishing her tea. My dad had taken the twins out for a while. The house was very quiet without them.

I looked out of the window at our little unkempt back garden. From behind me, against the huge, hugely significant silence of the house, the sound of my mum getting up from the kitchen table. Then the spoon clinked against the saucer as she placed her empty teacup on the drainer at my elbow. We stood side by side, looking out.

'It's a mess, isn't it,' she said. 'We're just not gardeners, I suppose.'

'It doesn't matter,' I said.

'No,' she said, turning to me, 'it doesn't matter.'

Then we were face to face. If I had a secret, I could never protect it from this. My mum was reading me, like a book. Not a child's book any longer, her expression was saying, but a story for young adults, with all the feelings, emotions and responsibilities falling into place like one word being placed perfectly in front of the other – one word, another, another, until I was revealed and my mum had read all she needed to know.

'Don't forget how much I love you,' she said, almost in a whisper.

'I won't forget, Mum, ever. I love you too.'

'That's good,' she said, holding onto me. 'Then that's all that matters. That's all I need.'

# ✲✲✲ Seventeen

**A**merica!

The first couple of gigs there took us right back to the beginning again. The venues were small, one like something from a film, with pool tables and a dining area, like a huge café, with too few people there to generate much excitement. We did okay though, once we started to do the high schools. Being in America together had excited us, with Leo's near-ecstatic delirium at seeing the States for the first time adding to our sense of occasion and achievement. Here we were, hopping from high school to college in so many small towns, heading eventually for San Francisco and then Los Angeles. Leo was going to lose his mind at the thought of going to LA. 'Ooh!' he kept gasping. 'Ooh! Ooh!'

We did a couple of local radio stations. There were too many of us to fit up with headphones and mikes in those little places, so we were going in two at a time sometimes. Leo and I went together, Ben and Angel, finally Kaylie and Miranda. Which seemed like a mistake to me, but they did all right. But all right was only all right – it wasn't good. We were always a bit too nerve-weary, worn down from coach rides bickering through west coast America. It all seemed too big and repetitively boring, our irritation somehow imposing itself on every view of expansive countryside, the sea, the massive sky. On radio we must have sounded like a bunch of tired tourists, happy to be there but overwhelmed by it all.

**✱✱✱**

Adam called me and called me. It was lovely. Or, as Adam would have said, it was beautiful. Being in America again was good, much better than the first time I was here. But being in America with Adam's hotline purring and ringing in my pocket every few hours was like – like nothing I could compare it to. We had spent that time together in Paris – romantic Paris – after the recording of our song, for the night before my return home.

Now here I was, along with all the others, hyper and bare-knuckled along the freeways of the West Coast, always only this far from a fist fight between the girls, with Ben ever super-cool in shades and Leo shaded-in with concern in one or the other corner of our mobile boxing ring. Everything was going crazy again. There was so much edge we were in constant danger of falling off.

Angel kept asking me how it went, with Adam in Paris. I didn't tell her anything, as I knew she'd only disapprove. She was like my mum in this respect: she could see the difference in me. The big difference between Angel and my mum, though, was that my mum was philosophical and accepting, where Angel looked peeved and went churlishly quiet.

The trouble with a tour like this, with so many other people, is that it's in your face the whole time. I had suffered from loneliness before, but now I suffered from lack of privacy. We all did. It's surprising how quickly everyone can get on everybody else's nerves. Kaylie and Miranda, best friends one minute, were at each other's throat the next.

'It's her,' one would say to me. 'You should hear what she went and said to Angel about me . . .'

'She says things,' the other would say. 'Do you want to know what she says about you?'

'I don't want to know,' I kept saying. I said it to Angel, time and time again. 'I wish they wouldn't keep trying to include me.'

'And me,' she said. 'Kaylie keeps telling me what Miranda says about me. And about you. Miranda's as bad. Especially about you.'

It was statements like that – 'especially about you' – that would kind of hit home, making me feel all prickly and defensive. She had become a friend, but she seemed a jealous one, demanding my full attention when I'd rather have chatted alone with Leo, or making faces at me whenever I was on the phone to Adam.

'You must take absolutely no notice,' Leo would be saying, when another fight would break out, things thrown, screams. A punch, sometimes. Plenty of long-hair-pulling.

Just before we were due to go one air, on our very first TV appearance together, all three Cats were spitting at each other, their arched back raised, sharp teeth showing.

'Keep it down!' Ben was ordering.

'Keep it down!' I tried to join in.

'You keep it down!' one of the girls hissed at me. 'You can't talk. Listen to her!'

'Listen to you.'

'Lovelies, come on now.'

'Sod off!'

'You!'

'No, you!'

'No, you!'

'No, you!'

'No! I said it first!'

'No you didn't!'

'Yes I did!'

'Didn't!'

'Did!'

'Didn't!'

'Did!'

'Oh, for –'

And all this as we were waiting to go live on air. Ben shut them up, in the end, because Leo couldn't do it. Leo was running backwards and forwards with his fingers in his ears as Ben shouted the girls down. I was laughing. I couldn't help it. Angel was smiling. We were all so tense, so wired, so tired. And we'd only just started!

But that level of hard-wired tension between performers is not always such a bad thing. When the TV producer worriedly waved us on, we started to perform as if we really meant it. The Cats were dancing at each other as if they were about to launch an attack. They came at me too, until I started to sing:

*Hurry up, hurry up*
*We ain't got much time.*
*I got my motor gunning*
*Like I'm doing Car Crime.*

I was, too: doing Car Crime, that is. We all were. The off-stage tension came into our on-stage performance, enhancing what we did with this edge of danger, as if we meant it, these crimes we were committing for the sake of our music.

*Tired of sittin' waitin'*
*'S gettin' all too much.*
*Feel like grinding thru my gears.*
*Feel like burning my clutch.*

That feeling of pent-up energy that spills out as anger and frustration rushed out of us on stage as we rushed at one another, not delivering lines so much as attacking with them. I remember thinking, or rather feeling, that this was the best way to deal with our difficulties, hoping that when the set was over, so then would be the friction.

It wasn't. It blundered on into the interview with us, so that nobody could concentrate on what was being said, but merely reacting with spontaneous anger.

'And how are you enjoying being in America?' The interviewer was called Evelyn Waugh, the early-evening chat-show hostess whose show this was.

'Are we in America?' Angel asked, blinking, looking about into the corners of the studio as if she was bemused by her surroundings. There was a live audience.

They didn't laugh.

'Sorry,' leapt in Miranda, 'she's a bit of a div.'

'A div? Does that mean the leader?'

'Hey!'

'Yeah, a div.'

'We don't really have a leader,' I tried to say.

'Did you call me a div?'

'We all know who the div is,' Kaylie said, as if she was speaking to the audience.

'Unless it's Ben,' I said, still trying to answer the question.

'So, Ben,' Evelyn said, 'you're the – div? Have I got that quite right?'

We all stopped. We were on TV in America and the glossy hostess was calling Ben a div! Ben, dark suit and tie, long hair, shades, never dropped a single degree of cool. He smiled and nodded.

The rest of us fell about laughing as Evelyn Waugh looked at us bemused, with a pretend half-smile on her face.

'That's right,' Ben said. 'I'm the div.'

We were falling about laughing.

'You guys are,' Evelyn struggled to say, 'you're, ah – you're kinda zany, aren't you?'

Leo was over the far side of the studio looking like he was just about to have kittens.

'That's right,' I said. 'We're all kinda zany. But Ben's the div. We'll never let him forget that either, will we, you zany guys.'

Evelyn was supposed to get to the bottom of what we were called.

'Amy Peppercorn and Car Crime featuring the Static Cats,' I answered.

'Who's who?' she tried to ask.

'Kaylie!' Kaylie said.

'Amy!'

'Miranda!'

'Angel!'

'Dave!'

'Div!'

That was it, we were lost. We fell to bits. Leo had a nice little litter of baby cats over the way, and Evelyn Waugh gave up on us with a shrug.

It was strange, the way we were biting bits out of one another one moment, the next we were the best and closest of friends. Especially Kaylie and Miranda. They were more like sisters. Then there was Angel and me. When she stopped trying to force me into some kind of opinion about someone or the other, when she relaxed, we went back to being good friends and young – by which I mean not worried and caring about next to nothing. Ben got on quite well with Dave, discussing music, listening to Dave's long, long line of madhouse experiences in the Biz. Ben was trying to learn from

Dave, I could tell. He wanted to have had Dave's experiences but was too young and impatient to wait for them.

Leo, you might think, would have to be on his own. No, of course not. Don't you know Lovely Leo better than that by now? Leo was with everyone. He would flit from place to place, from person to person like a butterfly. He was very lovely and very sweet. He asked me about Adam.

'We don't talk about that sort of thing!' Angel leapt in to say, whenever she was there to answer Leo's Adam-questions for me.

She listened to me on the phone to him; I know she did. Whenever he called me on the coach or in any hotel room I happened to be sharing with Angel, she'd grow very still and quiet with unspoken disapproval, until I found myself whispering into my mobile so that she wouldn't hear me. But she always heard, because she wanted to hear, but not to speak to me about it.

But just after our first TV appearance, things changed back to the way they were when we were first formed. We had a laugh. Ben was the div. He even seemed to like his new title. Kaylie and Miranda still fancied him like crazy, despite his newly acquired status.

Funny thing, though, our next gig was a bit of a lacklustre affair, with none of us turning on much of a performance. I don't know why; maybe we were each of us waiting for one of the others to inject some energy into the proceedings. At this rate we were unlikely to build up much of a following. Which is what you have to do in the States, or you go under – you disappear very quickly. America's such a nightmare pop market to break into for anyone from the UK. It never happens overnight. It's such a massive country, there's no real national press or TV or radio. Even the laws can change from one state to the next. So for a pop music act, each state is almost like starting over again from scratch. That's why it's necessary to keep coming back.

But for me, this was it. If we didn't crack America this time, I felt I would be confined to the UK and the rest of Europe – and now I wanted the whole thing, everywhere, the world!

It wasn't until we went on stage and nothing much happened did I realise how afraid I had been of nothing happening. 'Come on, Ben,' I hissed behind at him.

'What's going on tonight?'

'Get on with it then!' he hissed back at me. 'It's you lot. What's the matter with you?'

We went through the motions; that was all. Any audience, anywhere, would have picked up on our lack of commitment. Live performance is so much more than just singing the songs. It should be an experience, for everyone. It's more like a piece of theatre or a good film. It should make you feel for what's happening as if it's happening to you. But we lacked drama and tension.

When we came off stage that evening, everyone was subdued, even Leo, who looked at us all in turn, trying to spot what the matter was. None of us knew.

'What did you think,' I asked Angel, 'of what we did tonight?'

'I thought it was rubbish. Those two were all over the place, weren't they?' She was referring to Kaylie and Miranda. 'I think somebody should have a word with them, don't you?'

'Have a word? And say what?'

'Say what's most obvious. They were crap.'

'Oh,' I said, confused. 'I thought we – weren't we all a bit rubbish, don't you think?'

'You weren't,' Angel said.

She stopped there, almost as if she wanted to leave it open for me to say something. I felt I had to, because to say nothing would have been to suggest that Angel had been rubbish, where she said I had not. 'Neither were you,' I found myself reciting, as if the words had been handed to me on a slip of script-paper.

'You see what I mean then,' she said.

I glanced at Kaylie and Miranda where they reclined, splayed across a couple of coach seats each. What I hadn't realised, until that moment, was that Angel was looking over at them too. It was obvious that we were talking about them. From their faces, it looked like they understood and hated the fact that we were discussing them. They looked as if they knew what we'd been saying.

I looked away, which was probably the worst thing I could have done, to glance and then turn away. It must have appeared as a very dirty look.

Later on that day, Kaylie and Miranda were glancing at me and looking away with filthy faces. Angel spoke to them and they seemed all right. They looked it, anyway. I couldn't really tell. At least they weren't fighting, at the moment. But they still didn't seem to like the look of me.

Leo sidled over to me as I was trying to read a magazine. 'What on earth's going on with you girls?' he said.

I shook my head. 'I've no idea. I don't want anything to do with it.'

Leo tutted. 'What's happening to you, Amy? You're not usually like this?'

'Like this? Like what? What do you mean?'

'Lovely, Lovely,' he said, backing away a bit. 'Hey, hey. What's the matter? Why are you doing this?'

'Leo, again, this? What do you mean "this"? What am I

165

doing? I don't even know what it is I'm supposed to be doing.'

'Is it anything to do with Adam?' he said.

I had to look out of the window. America was winding by out there, as if it was the backdrop to an intense road-movie. The coach we were on supplied the soundtrack, Leo the dialogue. But it didn't make sense, this picture. Somewhere along the line the scriptwriters seemed to have lost their way. California looked lovely, if dry. Small towns did a very, very passable impression of the small towns of our TV screens, with large wooden houses with white fences, trucks, dusty garages with drugstores, farmers in pick-ups with dogs in the passenger seats. The road in this movie moved under us exactly reflecting the speed at which we were passing over it. Everything seemed in order. Everything, that is, except everything that was being said to me. 'Leo,' I said, 'I don't get it. What's supposed to be happening?'

'Sweet,' he said, 'I don't know. That's what I'm trying to find out. There seems to be such an atmosphere brewing.'

'I know that much,' I said. 'But I don't understand it. Perhaps you'd better ask Angel?'

'I have. She said I should ask you. Miranda said to ask Kaylie. Kaylie suggested I speak to Angel. Angel sent me here, and here you are trying to send me straight back again.'

'Well, what does Ben say then?'

'He doesn't say anything.'

'Then neither do I,' I said, looking out of the window again.

# ***★ Eighteen

**N**one of the tension went away. When we went on stage that evening, it was all still there. And this was our biggest venue yet: a big county high school between two fairly large towns.

During that afternoon, *Love Makes Me Sick* had come on the radio in the coach. My initial excitement soon drained away when I saw the reaction of the Cats. Leo leapt, Ben and Dave grinned, but the Cats scratched at the furniture, snarling at the obvious fact that this was an Amy Peppercorn song and they didn't appear in it. The high school venue to which we were headed was where Amy Peppercorn and Car Crime were appearing: only incidentally featuring the Static Cats. I hadn't thought too much about it, until now. Now I could see how catty the girls, including Angel, were going to get over this. There was nothing I could do about it, especially with one of my songs getting radio play. Poking out my tongue or sticking up a finger at the Cats couldn't have had a worse effect.

The publicity machine behind our tour was cranking up, giving us far more exposure than I'd had on my first American visit.

'There's a Ray Ray and Pierre Piatta influence working behind the scenes,' Leo whispered to me.

The scenes they were working behind were the ever more severe bickering of Angel, Kaylie, Miranda and me. It didn't seem to matter to anyone that my song on the radio would most likely translate into bigger and better audiences. Egos can be so very destructive. I wanted to speak to Angel, on her own, to find out why she was so happy to be so mean to me, after the friendly way in which we had started out. Why had she changed?

I wanted to speak to Angel, but she evidently didn't want to talk to me. Nobody wanted to speak to anybody else. We got ready in silence, until I switched on the radio to break up the oppressive atmosphere a bit.

'She's after hearing herself again!' one of the others said.

It was such a stupid, snide remark I decided to ignore it. Only the oppressive air reverberated with my refusal to be drawn in, as if I was placing myself ever further above the others. I wasn't, believe me. It wasn't like that, not for me. It was horrible and I wanted it to end.

But it didn't end, not yet, anyway. We had to make our way to the stage and wait in frustration and tension to be introduced:

'All the way from England,' the announcer announced, 'Amy Peppercorn!'

It made me breathe in and hold my breath.

'And Car Crime!'

No exhalation yet, no respite.

'Featuring – the Standing Cats!'

I almost choked. So did the Cats.

But we were now facing a pretty good crowd, with the biggish auditorium of the huge school hall something well over three quarters full. Not bad, considering how little they knew of us. We should have been at our synergetic best for our biggest and liveliest American live show yet. Our stage set should have been gathering momentum to enhance the reputation being built behind the scenes by the English and the French and the American publicity machines. We, however, seemed to want to take another path than the one being laid down for us. We came out onto that stage in single file, angry and upset and full of spite.

Yes, things were getting spiteful. I didn't want it that way. We were all dressed in red and white, with angry red or white spiteful faces. Ben was coldly impervious to our gripes and grapples. Leo tried his best to pretend that nothing was going wrong. He started us up.

*Hurry up, hurry up*
*We ain't got much time.*
*I got my motor gunning*
*Like I'm doing Car Crime.*

We were each of us guilty, in one way or another, but all claiming innocence, each blaming the other for what was going wrong. The Cats spat in a pack behind me. I looked round. Miranda rushed at me. I dodged away. She sang:

*Tired of sittin' waitin'*
*'S gettin' all too much.*
*Feel like grinding thru my gears.*
*Feel like burning my clutch.*

Kaylie came up and pushed Miranda. They tried to turn their dance into a fight. Angel danced between them and turned the fight back into a dance. I sang:

*We're going nowhere,*
*But lookin' good while we get there.*
*So follow if you dare,*
*To destination anywhere –*

I should be able to say, at some point here, that we sang, the whole group of us; only we didn't. The singing might have coincided when it should, during the coming and going of chorus and verse, but we were not – we were never together enough to be considered harmonious, not with such acrimony and deep-seated resentment pitting us one against the other. And that is exactly what we were, four individuals, or two or three factions waging war on stage, confronting one another in dance, blasting lyrics into the opposite face like a well-aimed punch:

*We're both out on a roll, runnin' out of control,*
*Hold me, don't let me go!*

Miranda grabbed me by the shoulder right at the end there, and tried to throw me behind her. I may be small, but I tell you I'm stocky and solid-set enough to resist being pushed around by the likes of her. She soon found herself pushed back. Kaylie screamed at me.

But the crowd, our audience, screamed louder, drowning out whatever it was Kaylie was trying to shout me down with. Suddenly, as flash quick as the speed of light, we felt the electrified energy of the whole hall lighting us up, firing us with the adrenalin of the fight.

'Now!' Ben cried out. 'Now! Do it! Do it!'

I knew what it was.

'Now!' he shrieked at me.

With Miranda looking as if she was about to try to come back and hit me, with the audience pumping up like the crowd around a fist fight, fight, fight, fight, I took the mike. My feet were planted hard against the boards of the stage for what I had to do. It must have looked as if I was squaring up to defend myself against the assault of the wail of the Cats.

The crowd, jostling forward against the stage, raised their fists in a call to arms. I looked out. I breathed, deeply, deeply.

It was shocking! I'd screamed in concert before, many times, but never with such ferocity. We were all shocked by it, with the exception perhaps of Ben, who seemed to catch the dreadfulness and spin it, doing a hand-brake turn with a screech of burning tyres and a slam of the gearbox and roar of the engines. I swear there was blue smoke in the air and the dying rubber smell of a road race in and out of the super-market car park in the dead of night.

Car Crime was back. No Amy Peppercorn to speak of, not featuring Cats static but felines in motion: four of us speed-ing across the stage as Ben and Dave and Leo took us for the ride of a lifetime. Everything I'd ever felt on stage – the elation, the joy, the love – they didn't enter here. I was scared. I laughed out loud, as I would have in the back of a fast car doing way, way over the odds. The others, the girls, were as afraid as I was. We all laughed. We screamed. All four of us together gathered to cry out across the packed heads pooled around us, spreading out from the stage but driving forward, pressing with all the centrifugal force of our accelera-tion. This couldn't last for long. Nobody can accelerate at this rate without soon meeting trouble in the form of a brick wall or an oncoming vehicle. This was too dangerous. Some of the people in the audience were scrambling onto the stage, only to fly back off, not crowd-surfing but more like attacking from above.

Angel screamed. She took me and dashed with me to the front of the stage while Ben cranked the energy levels up still further, gathering sound momentum from I don't know where, driving us on, Angel and me, to scream into the faces closest to the stage as they cried back, scrambling for more and more height. I found myself hand in hand with the Angel of doom, a wild anti-angelic figure flinging lightning bolts by my side. For the moment I looked into her face, I was sure those Cats'-eyes were greenly feline, very nearly glowing with envy.

It was a vision that halted me. I slowed everything down. Well, somebody had to. Ben was in communication with me, I realised. He had all the while been gauging the performance, the vitality, wildness of energy, from me. So that was what he did. He bounced off of me, so that if I was uninspired, the whole thing fell flat. It was a huge responsibility, but when the time came to keep the lid on this, I took the lead and slowed us down, pulling us not quite to a halt, but to another starting point.

*Hurry up, hurry up*
*We ain't got much time.*
*I got my motor gunning*
*Like I'm doing Car Crime.*

Now, though, with the blue-smoked energy within us nowhere near expended, *Destination Anywhere* looked to a new anywhere to which we and our audience were destined, where anywhere could become everywhere, the collective somewhere containing everyone, always.

*Come with me, run with me,*
*Laugh and have fun with me.*
*Tell me now, what do you say?*
*There's nowhere to hide with me,*
*Take a joy ride with me,*
*Nothing can stand in our way!*

*We're going nowhere,*
*But lookin' good while we get there.*

*So follow if you dare,*
*To destination anywhere.*
*We're both out on a roll, runnin' out of control,*
*Hold me, don't let me go!*

The song ended there, usually. Not this time though, not this time. 'Hurry up! Hurry up!' I yelled out over all the heads. '*Love Makes Me Sick!*' I cried.

However many times I'd done this song, it had never come out like this. And so it was with everything we did, driving roughshod over all that had gone before, speeding forward into the wildly changing perspective of the future. Whatever was there before, we ripped apart and reconstructed it more dangerously, using every bit of friction the factions between us had created every day in close confinement together. The disquiet and frustration we all felt came out, channelled into a new creative energy I wasn't sure I liked entirely, but which I knew full well I could easily become addicted to, like a drug.

There was no stopping us: the genie was out of the bottle and was too energetic to be put back and denied.

Even Leo was affected along with the rest of us. We had come off stage much more of a group than when we went on. Electrical charge seemed to bond us together, but soon to separate us like static and stand our hair on end. Certainly, even Leo's curly mop swung quite straight as he lashed out with a pillow when we four girls cornered and clobbered him. Miranda caught me in the eye with the corner of a pillowcase as Leo ran out of the room. It was an accident, but I saw the satisfaction in her own eye as mine set wildly to watering.

Dave the guitarist and Ben were there, trying to be cool. We soon knocked off their dark glasses and Ben chased Kaylie and then Miranda across the twin beds of his and Dave's room, until Miranda conspired to get caught and the two of them went over in a rough tussle but with more than a couple of quick kisses from Miranda. Kaylie started to cry and claimed that Ben had hurt her shoulder.

'He wasn't anywhere near you,' Angel insisted.

'Did I hurt you?' Ben said.

Kaylie offered him her arm. Ben kissed it. Miranda smacked Kaylie round the back of the head too hard with quite a hefty pillow and they were off, screaming and scratching, with Angel hovering over them pretending to split them up but managing, slyly, to goad them on.

'Sweethearts,' Leo came back in crying, 'we've been asked to keep the noise down, or leave the hotel. As it's well after midnight –'

Kaylie and Miranda launched a united attack upon poor Leo, catching him mid-riff, mid-sentence. He let out an 'Oof!' before trying to continue.

'As it is after midnight, can I suggest that we all – please, stop! We'll get thrown out of the hotel. Ben, please. Dave!'

'Come on,' I said. 'Come on, that's enough.'

Which was enough to launch the you're-not-in-charge routines again, painting cats' faces on the Cats, feline expressions asking, who-did-I-think-I-was, or worse. It was enough, though, to put an end to our fun and games for another night, dispersing us and sending each to his or her own shared room.

I was with Angel as ever, falling into a by now familiar routine of teeth and face cleaning in turns to keep out of each other's way in the bathroom.

Angel had a way of jumping into bed like a little girl. 'Different tonight,' she said, bouncing, 'or what?'

'Different?'

'The performance. Give them something to write about in their papers, eh?'

There had been a press presence, four or five cameras flashing, which was quite an amount for us so far in America. They had attempted to get an interview with us afterwards, in the dressing rooms. 'We're Car Criminals!' Angel had shrieked at them. 'We're Static Cats! We're desperadoes!'

'She's Amy Peppercorn,' Leo had interjected.

'I'm a Car Criminal!' I screamed with Angel, with Kaylie, with Miranda. 'We're together!'

'Were we together?' I had to ask Angel, as I crept into my bed. 'I didn't get it. It was like one big fight.'

'Don't worry about it,' Angel said.

'I'm not worried,' I said. 'It's just that –'

But my mobile went off and I was out of bed and into the bathroom to take it so that nobody else but the caller would be able to hear what I was saying.

She was still awake, even though the call had been of record length, starting on one level, in one mood, finishing on another mood level entirely. Angel must have sensed or simply seen the change in me as I emerged, as she said, 'You're looking all nice and flushed.'

'Am I?'

'Am I?' she mimicked, in a dreamy voice. 'Course you are. Look at you.'

I climbed back into bed. Half the time, since we'd been in America, I'd managed to avoid sharing a room with anyone. Sharing had been enjoyable, at first, but had turned into a burden, an invasion of the privacy I hadn't quite realised I prized so highly. I wanted not to have to retreat into the bathroom to speak to Adam. I wanted not to be inspected before the call, after it, then to have to account for the changes. It was nobody's business but mine. Mine and Adam's. Adam's and mine, with nobody else involved. That was how we spoke, one to the other, as if we were together, alone, concerned for nothing much more than how we felt about . . . about how we felt. The way Adam felt about how I felt made me feel more like how he felt. Which sounds confusing, because it was. Confusing, exciting, and beautiful. Like a brilliant blue stone, a mineral that by all experience should never have been that colour. Like lapis lazuli.

'Look at you,' Angel went on, 'always got that thing stuck round your neck.'

I touched the stone to my throat.

'Always touching it, as if it meant something. I know what,' she was saying, with her Angel-face hardening against me, 'I know what you've gone and done. You've gone and let him in, haven't you?'

'Angel,' I said.

'I know you have. It's obvious.'

'Look,' I said, 'I don't think it's got anything to do with you. So I'd be grateful if you'd just – if you'd just –'

Trying not to be too rude or aggressive towards her, I was struggling to find what to say.

'You fool!' she said, as I struggled on.

'Angel,' I said, 'what is the matter with you? What does it matter to you what I do when –'

'Of course it matters!'

'Why?'

'Because – because you're one of my best friends!'

I halted, barely concealing a smile. Best friends? From what

I knew of Angel and her catty list of 'friends', it wasn't necessarily a good thing to be one of the best.

'What friends?' I said.

'Oh, charming!'

'No,' I said, allowing out that smile, 'listen, it's just that you're always being so – sometimes I don't think you even like me.'

'Don't you? I just hate – no, it doesn't matter. I care about what happens to you. You've been hurt before, I know.'

'And I sometimes wish I'd never told you about it.'

'Oh, charming again!' she said, throwing herself down on the mattress, turning away and covering herself up at the same time. 'You're determined to insult me tonight, aren't you?'

'No, Angel. Come off it. You know I –'

'Oh, I know,' she said, still facing the wall. 'Forget it. I will.'

'No,' I said, 'no – come on, it's not like that. You know how confused I am, sometimes. We're always fighting with each other.'

'All right,' she said.

But it wasn't. It wasn't all right. 'Angel?' I said, after a while. The lights were out by this time, but neither of us was sleeping. 'I know you're awake. I want to talk to you. Can I talk to you?'

'I need to go to sleep. We're doing the mall in the morning.'

'I know what we're doing in the morning. Please don't. Just talk to me for a while, would you?'

'What about?'

'About – you say I'm your friend.'

'I don't know if you're my friend, do I? I only know I'm your friend.'

'Yes. That's what you say.'

'I am. If only you knew.'

'Knew what? Why do you say such things?'

She sat up, finally. 'Amy,' she said, 'I'm your friend. I look out for you. It isn't easy.'

'How do you mean, look out for me?'

'I just do. You don't get it. You're just – ah, forget it. Just forget it.' And she went back under, burrowing beneath her covers where I couldn't get at her, as if hiding, hiding away from me.

# *⃰*⃰⃰⃰Nineteen

**W**e were to play at a shopping mall. It was new; they were just opening it. We were going there to do a couple of songs only. It was a good gig though, as there were to be lots of reporters and a couple of TV companies.

After breakfast, we had just eighty or ninety miles to go: no distance at all. A couple of hours maybe, that was all. You'd have thought, in that short space of time, we wouldn't have had enough opportunity to get on each other's nerves. You'd be way wrong though. After last night, Angel seemed strung out, too nervy not to get on to anybody else. Half an hour or so was all it took for the first screaming match to start.

Ben was huddled near the front of the coach with Dave. Dave had a terrible hangover. He looked as if he might be contemplating being sick at any moment. Ben looked a bit worse for wear too, but not as pasty-white as Dave. I was hoping that Ben wasn't being led into the kind of life with Dave that he probably wouldn't be able to handle. When the girls kicked off, Dave looked even more startlingly ill and Ben's face disappeared into his hands.

'You can talk!' Miranda was scrapping with Angel.

Most of the time it was impossible to follow the line of any argument, once it got going. It always consisted of insults and veiled references to things that may or may not have happened in the past.

'Stop!' Miranda shrieked at the top of her voice.

The driver up the front behind the covering curtain slammed on the brakes and halted us, as he believed he'd been ordered so to do. It was an emergency with half the passengers standing as we stopped, with the bus decelerating way more suddenly than its contents.

Ben and I had been hurrying away from Dave as his breakfast hurried away from him, with Miranda standing a bit further up and Angel a bit further still. A stray sound man was asleep on the back bench seat: the roadies usually made their own way from gig to gig, leaving early in a couple of beaten-up vans.

There was no real emergency, until we stopped for one. Grinding to a halt like that created a crisis with everyone tumbling and falling towards the front where Dave's street pizza steamed full ahead waiting colourfully for slip, slide, slither and fall. And fall we did, everything over clash of elbow and head and shoulder all in a crunch and crumple on Dave's anointed floorspace. We went down in a heap: me, Ben, Miranda, Angel. Kaylie bashed her nose on the seat in front of where she was sitting.

Everyone was screaming, but no one louder or more hysterically than Leo. He hadn't been thrown anywhere, sitting in his seat belt up front with the driver as he was. He had turned to see what all the commotion was, thrusting his head through the opening in the curtains, only to be confronted by the spectre of Kaylie, with half her face and a good part of her upper body covered in a rich red bib as she staggered towards him.

With the rest of us, excluding Dave and the sound man who had disappeared, in a jumbled, bespattered heap on the floor, Kaylie bubbled forth wailing, dripping, her eyes already puffing up, the teeth in her open mouth stained pink against raw gums and bubbly red tongue.

'Oh my God!' Leo screamed – yes, he literally screamed. 'Whatever have you – oh my! Quick! Oh no!' And he tried to fling himself into the back of the coach, only to find the seatbelt binding him fast to the front.

The rest of us were untangling our limbs and trying to stand up, slipping and sliding one on the other as Leo leapt from the front and sent us all scattering again. Kaylie fell on Leo, collapsing against him, and she and he fell into the same spot so recently vacated by the rest of us. Dave was trying to apologise, Kaylie had almost passed out, Leo and the other two Cats were wailing and Ben was dragging everyone up and planting them safely on seats. I found myself strangely detached from the scene, somehow able to watch it all from somewhere above, maybe from one of the luggage racks.

'That's your fault, that is!' Miranda seemed to be scratching up at me.

'No it isn't!' Angel was saying. 'It's yours!'

'Mine?'

'Help me,' said Leo, cradling Kaylie, his face especially whitened against the brilliance of red that Kaylie was anointing him with.

'Look!' Ben shouted. 'She's hurt!'

'I'm so sorry,' said Dave. 'Oh, my head.'

As he said that, I realised what it was with my own head. It was revolving. I was up on the ceiling, viewing all the activity swirling away from below me in sickness and life's leaking scarlet. 'Oh,' I uttered. 'Oh. Oh!'

'It's never my fault! It's hers! What's the matter with her?'

Kaylie was coming round, gazing at all the confusion with deeper confusion in her eyes. She looked up at me.

'Water,' Ben was saying. 'Where's my water?'

Below me, someone was holding Ben's water in tiny, far-away hands: it was me. That was my lap way down there where I was sitting. Something told me I'd forgotten to take my epilepsy medication that day, but my hands were too far away now to do anything about it.

'She's got it!' Miranda was saying to someone about someone else.

Our driver appeared with cubes of ice, wrapping them, applying the wrap to Kaylie's face.

'What's going on?' the sound man yawned, rising from the floor behind me as if he was getting out of bed first thing in the morning. 'What's happening?'

Everyone else was screaming, silently, from tiny, roundly open mouths, from far, far away.

The coach was an absolute mess. There were clothes and stuff everywhere, like a big mobile boot sale. As we were playing a mall with no changing rooms, we'd left the hotel wearing our performance outfits. All of which were ruined by – you know. I'm sure you don't need any more of those kinds of details. The outcome of it all was that we had to drag out our luggage from the special compartment, changing into whatever came to hand as the driver started up again, setting off far too suddenly, sending us all scuttling to the back, clutching for a hand hold or falling again, but not quite so disastrously this time.

Kaylie had two black eyes and a badly swollen nose. It might have been broken. She should have had a doctor look at her. And so should I. There was a lump at the back of my head the size of a bird's egg in the nest of my hair. I took my medication and drank gallons of water and began to feel much better. But we were all bumped and bruised in one way or another, and there were no doctors, so we carried on.

Our clothes were all over the place – not those in the coach, but the ones we were wearing. We had to fish them out of the jumble and just sling them on. The hairstyles and make-up we'd left the hotel with got left behind, lost in the tangle heap of hair and harm after the accident. We improvised on the rest of the journey, cleaning up as best we could.

Leo was in favour of phoning through to try to cancel the gig. But the road crew, who always went ahead early, would be setting up by now, and none of us wanted not to perform. We were shaken up, especially Kaylie, but we felt like real troupers now, coping with everything the road could throw at us. We all felt wobbly, a little sick, but at least it had stopped all the arguments, for the time being.

As we were that late, the road crew had finished the set by the time we arrived and the presenters on stage were ad-libbing, trying and failing to be funny in front of a mall filled with a more and more restless crowd. We ran on.

'Amy Peppercorn!' one of the presenters managed to shout as we appeared.

Angel grabbed a mike. 'The Static Cats!' she shouted into the crowd, most of which consisted of moms with little kids, a few dads scattered here and there.

A couple of groups of grunge skateboarders booed.

'We're Car Crime!' I shouted now, into the mike next to Angel.

The grungers cheered.

We launched into our first song. There was going to be a speech by the town's mayor after our set. But the audio boys had had time to do an excellent job. We sounded pretty good. We looked like a rabble. The skaters liked that. Kaylie came forward to sing, thrusting her damaged face out into the crowd as if she were wearing some kind of badge of honour. Some of the mums didn't care much for that, I could see, but the skaters seemed to be growing in number, starting to take over the available space, crowding forward to get a better look at us. Miranda had a bandanna tied half over her face. It looked silly on the bus, but suddenly it was just the thing. With the clothes we were wearing, the strung-out look on our guitarist's face, Ben's cool, Leo's flamboyancy, Kaylie's black eyes, our whole confrontational stage-style, we started to kick ass. I say that, because that's what Angel decided to scream out across the crowded face of the families looking up at us. 'We kick ass!'

'Car Crime!' Kaylie cried, black eyed and alarmingly beautiful.

'We're Car Crime – we kick ass!' Miranda booted across the stage, with one eye hidden, her white boxer shorts showing above the low waistline of her jeans. She'd never worn jeans on stage, especially not like that. She had undone them at the front to let them fall down a lot.

This was something else. Some of the families and the organisers might not have liked it, but the skaters and their friends and their friends loved it. So did we. Our two songs were sung but we were not done, neither was our audience done with us. For they went from crowd to audience in a song, easily in two, till by track four we were kickin' and they were too and the mall was calling all the way to Echo Beach and back, on bikes, on boards, or on-board with the windows wound down and the wind up and the surf ready to ride and all and every good time image coming out to be realised in the town's new shopping mall where the mayor was quietly awaiting his turn.

His face was a picture, what I could see of it. I couldn't see much, because I wasn't looking, not with an all-time good-time performance such as this to be enjoyed. The lump in my hair hatched and a firebird flew out of the back of my head. We were kickin', out on a roll, running out of control. TV cameras were following as Leo's face was glowing as our reputation was growing. Kaylie Blackeyes was crowing. The adrenalin was flowing.

We were Car Crime. We kicked. You better believe it – you bet!

'I don't quite get it,' I said to Adam over the phone that night. 'The more we fight, or the more injured we are, the better we get.'

I was lying on the bed in a single room, enjoying my own company for once. The others, including Kaylie, with two black eyes and a badly swollen nose from the accident, had all gone to town to soak up the atmosphere we'd created for ourselves. A fall like that would normally get people down; with us, it did the reverse. Shake us up a bit, and all we did was fly round all the harder. Ben didn't go with them though; I think he wasn't feeling too good, but not because of the accident. He wasn't like Dave, who was up for it, whatever, whenever. Ben wanted Dave's experience but lacked Dave's cast-iron constitution. Ben always had to suffer the consequences. Dave was always smoking, cigarettes, and other, more wacky stuff. Ben didn't do that, I was happy to see; he just joined in the drinking every now and then, but wasn't much good at it.

'If it wasn't for Ben,' I told Adam, 'we'd be pulling each other to bits by now. The Cats and I would be tearing each other's hair out.'

'For what?' he asked.

He melted me. I'd lain down to speak to him, but tensely,

lying looking up at the hotel ceiling from the hotel bed, with the lump on the back of my head pressed gingerly into three piled pillows. My telephone had gone off almost as soon as I'd got settled. As it rang, as I read the words that told me it was Adam calling, I reached automatically for the blue stone resting at the base of my throat.

He melted me. If I was hardening against the continuous brawl of us all as we toured those school halls and shopping malls, Adam was becoming the antidote. As we spoke, I felt myself soften, relaxing into piles of not so soft hotel pillows and particularly lumpy quilts.

'For what?' he asked: for what would we be tearing out each other's hair?

'I can't answer that. I wish I could. There's just so much tension between us. We didn't start out like that.'

'Ah,' he said, 'the end is never so like the beginning, is it?'

'No,' I smiled, 'the end is never so like the beginning. It's a shame.'

'But it gives you a better performance?'

'That's the weird thing. The more we fight, the more we find out what else we can do. It's kind of creative, if you can understand what I mean?'

'I think so. It is the energy. It has to come from somewhere. On tour, it is so difficult to keep on. It tires you out, no?'

'It does. But you're right – we fight and all the energy levels come up. Then – then they disappear again. The adrenalin comes and goes. And when it goes, it leaves me drained, emptied out, finished. I've had it, tonight.'

'Then I should go, perhaps?'

'No, no. I didn't mean that. Don't go. Adam, I need this. Talk to me. Talk to me all night. I've got more fighting to do tomorrow. I need – I need you, Adam.' I stopped. I stopped breathing.

He breathed. 'You need me?'

'Yes. Yes, I think I – you know Adam, I feel like – like I'm – I just can't say it.'

He was listening to me intently. If he had been here, I knew he would be looking at me, extra-seriously. 'Don't say it,' he whispered. 'No, you don't have to say it.'

# **Twenty**

I felt beautiful. After such a perfect night's sleep, after such a telephone conversation, nothing could get to me. On such a morning!

'You're looking rather flushed and wonderful today,' Leo welcomed me at breakfast. Nobody else was there. 'I expect I'll have to go and rouse them,' Leo said, as I looked over the breakfast tables, noting the complete lack of familiar faces. 'I left them to it last night. It was a celebration of something or the other, though I never quite managed to discover what.'

'Just, maybe, being alive?' I suggested.

'After the accident yesterday, you mean?' he said. 'I know, it was terrible. It made me feel quite –'

'No,' I said, 'I mean just being alive.'

'Oh, my,' Leo fawned. 'We are in touch with the sheer beauty of the world this morning, are we not? And what, pray, lovely maiden, has brought on this lust for life, all of a sudden?'

'It's not all of a sudden,' I said, feeling warm, relaxed and happy. 'I've thought this through, Leo.'

'I'm happy to hear it,' he said, reaching out, taking my hand from the top of the table. 'Just don't forget,' he said, seriously, 'it's still a man's world out there.'

'In here it's not,' I said, laying my hand over my heart, with the brilliant blue pendant hanging between the spread of my fingers.

'And that,' said Leo, 'is the heart of the matter. The crux of the problem.'

'Leo, there is no problem.'

He squeezed my hand. 'Are you sure, Lovely? Are you so sure?'

I nodded, smiling. 'If you could only hear how he speaks to me,' I said. If Leo could hear how Adam declared his feeling in terms of the beauty he wanted in his life; if only Leo could feel how I felt, understanding on the same level as I understood Adam, as he understood me, then he wouldn't be squeezing his doubts so firmly into my hand. My hand, my head, my heart was sure now: had been so, in fact, for some time. All I had to do was allay my doubts and fears and set my emotions free to let myself feel how I now felt. I had only to hear Adam tell me he loved me – me, and only me – and I was set free of apprehension and guilt from the past, free to love him back. 'If you only heard him, Leo, you would understand.'

'Oh, sweet, I understand, believe me. If there's one thing I do, it's understand. And I care.'

'And you worry,' I said.

'Sweet,' he said, very seriously, 'look at everything. Look at what we're doing. All the fighting, the passions, the performances. Everything bubbles over all the time. If you could have seen the others last night, out celebrating with nothing in particular to celebrate, except a coach crash.'

'It wasn't a crash, Leo. Don't exaggerate.'

'Exaggerate? Me?' He laughed. 'No, everything's exaggerated in this pop world, especially on a tour like this. That's what I mean.'

'I know, Leo.'

'Lovely,' he said, with his face clouding over, 'I have to know that you know. The way you feel now, it cannot possibly be trusted.'

'I do know, Leo.'

He halted. All the clouds cleared from his face. A smile came out. Leo could have cried then, if he'd allowed himself. 'I've missed you,' he said.

'Oh, Leo,' I said, hugging him. I always hugged Leo. He me. We were like that, especially when we were together. But he was right: we hadn't been talking together, alone together, not nearly enough. It saddened me that we hadn't had enough heart-to-hearts, not enough girl-talk, not nearly enough hugs. 'I've missed you too,' I said. 'Thank you for caring about me.'

'Oh, don't thank me. I'm happy enough, if you are. Are you?'

'What do you think?' I asked, smiling at him, smiling for him, to show how happy I was.

'Then I'm happy,' as he hugged me again. 'Now, I must go and rouse the rabble, or we'll never get anywhere today. The blue stone suits you, by the way,' he said. It was the first time he'd referred to it since Adam had given it to me in Paris.

I had been touching it without realising: something I did quite often, or so it would seem.

'Yes,' I said. 'Adam gave it to me for my birthday.'

'Yes, I know,' he said.

'He's coming over,' I said.

'Coming over? Here?'

'Next week. To see me. For the end of the tour.'

'Good. Good. You're pleased. You touch the blue stone when you're pleased.'

'Lapis lazuli.'

'Oh yes, of course. It looks lovely. Better on your throat than dangling on Miranda's ears. He should have given you the whole set.'

'The set?'

'Necklace and earrings.'

'Oh.'

'You didn't give them to her, did you? He did, didn't he?'

'Who?'

'Adam?'

'Oh – oh, yes. He did. How did you know?'

'I – someone must have told me. Why, was it a secret?'

'No – no!'

'Lovely, what's the matter? Didn't you –'

'Leo,' I grinned, 'nothing's the matter. Don't start worrying about me again. Go and get the others together. We've got a long way to go.'

'Yes, and a big concert tonight.'

'With any luck, they'll all sleep all the way there.'

'We should be so lucky, eh?'

We laughed. Leo left. I kept the broad smile stretched across my face until it was too heavy to hold. It was soon too heavy to hold.

No luck. Nobody slept. They were wrecked, partied to bits, but that only seemed to wind up the whole claustrophobic atmosphere of the hot and smelly and too-small coach. It wasn't much more than an extended van, really, a removals truck with seats and party people in, with cheap fabric cushions on plastic-backed chairs. The air reeked of hot plastic and spot cream and feet and yesterday's burgers. It felt like another, nastier accident was about to happen. We were boxed for hours and hours in gloom, peering out of unwashed windows as if through a fug of fog, at a blurred America brought into focus only at the end of each journey with the concentrated energy of live performance and animated audience. Shut in like this, it was no wonder we bickered, arguing and fighting over everything and nothing.

They were all very, very good at getting on my nerves. Every one of them. Maybe not Leo. Or Ben. Not Dave so much. Or our driver, who was more or less an anonymous entity curtained off from us, keeping himself very much to himself every day and night. No, it was the girls. Every one of them. They were expert at doing all they could to get at everyone. What did they do? They just had to speak, to whisper, to look, spying out, out of the corner of a Cat's-eye, bitching about everything and nothing.

The worst thing though, the very worst, was that she was wearing them. It may or may not have been my imagination playing tricks on me, but wasn't she flaunting those little blue buttons dangling from her lobes? Miranda was in the habit of collapsing into a chair rather than simply sitting down. Whenever she fell, her hair fell back, exposing fully the coincidence of lapis lazuli in her ears. She seemed to be – she did seem to be – going out of her way to show them to me. Time and again she flicked back her hair to drink water, or tucked her hair behind her ears. Had she ever done that, before today? I didn't think so. I'd certainly never noticed it before. Or the smug expression she wore every time she glanced away from me. Which was often, as I kept catching her glances as they nipped away in the other direction, her attention alternating between my face and whatever else. There was always something else. I glanced, she glanced away. I glanced again, away she went, with a sway of blue stone under the sweep of her hair.

Leo had tried to attract my attention on numerous occasions. After the initial happiness of my morning, I couldn't have coped with his concerned questions, his care. The possibility of having to explain anything to him weighed me down, along with the details of what I'd have to say. I couldn't have said it, not after making out I knew Adam was supposed to have given Miranda the earrings. So I avoided him, disappearing into my private thoughts, with some isolating earphones plugged in and turned up loud. I was trying not to hear anything of what was going on around me. My eyes were closed half the time. If I pretended to go to sleep, I wouldn't have to see Miranda throwing her hair back at me, showing me her ears – the blue swinging flash of the stones that I felt should have been hanging where only my plugged earphones blared. But every time I opened my eyes, Miranda looked quickly away. Every time!

In the end I shifted over next to the window, to look out instead of in, at America passing rather than the fast passage of emotions flitting like the coloured particles of light on the insides of my eyelids. Someone came and dumped themselves beside me. I was quite hoping it would be Leo, but the weight and fall of the slump on the next seat told me that it wasn't him. I hoped it wasn't Miranda.

It wasn't. It was Angel. As I looked at her she started to speak to me. The music I'd plugged into my ears wouldn't allow me to hear what she was saying. I watched her mouth move for a few moments, wishing I could keep it like that, mouths moving without sound or meaning. Nobody would let me get away with it; they spoke, I had to listen.

'. . . between you and her,' Angel was saying as I

disconnected myself, as my private sounds stopped and connected me back to the public words coming at me.

'What's going on?'

'What? I couldn't hear you.'

'What is it with you and her this morning?' Angel asked, without trying to indicate to whom she was referring. 'What's going on now?'

'Now?'

'There's always something going on,' she said.

'Yeah, you're telling me. Always.'

'So what is it now?'

'Who says there's anything going on?'

'She does.'

'Oh. Does she? What does she have to say?'

'You keep giving her filthy looks all the time. You keep on doing it, every few minutes.'

'She says that, does she?'

'And you do. I've seen you doing it.'

'Yeah, well, we're all getting on each other's nerves.'

'Is that all it is then? Is that why you keep –'

'No. It isn't. There's something else. I really don't want to talk about it.'

'No?'

'No.'

'Oh.' And she sat looking about, out of the window, back at Miranda, out of the window, back. 'He bought them for her, then?' she said, as if from nowhere.

I stiffened in my seat, saying nothing.

Angel turned to face me. 'You know he gave them to her, don't you? It was a set. Earrings and necklace.'

She knew, as if she had known all along, what was bothering me. 'How did you know?' I said. 'I thought you told me –'

'I didn't tell you anything. I didn't know. Somebody told me.'

'I don't believe you.'

'No, I can't remember who told me.'

'No, not that. That it was a set. I don't believe you. You're lying.'

'Me? Me? I'm not lying. I'm only telling you what I was told. Why am I lying?'

'I don't know why you're lying. Why does anybody lie?'

'To hell with you! I don't have to take this!'

'No! Neither do I!' I was saying as she shot away, stomping off as far from me as she could get. Which wasn't far: certainly not far enough.

From then on it was dirty looks between Miranda and me, Angel and me; one, the other, one, the other. Kaylie joined in at one point, chucking looks about between us all until we were a boiling pot bubbling and burning with the lid on, all set to burst.

We went on. On we went until Angel could bear it no longer and she was swooping back down on me like an angel of doom with looks like black wings. She flapped back down into the seat beside me. 'Look!' she started. 'Look! I'm not bothered, right? It's not me, I'm not bothered. Right?'

'Right.'

'So don't call me a liar.'

'All right. You're not a liar.'

'Right. I'm supposed to be your friend.'

'Are you?'

'Aren't I? I always thought I was. You're the unfriendly one, don't forget, not me. You're the one always trying to get a single room instead of sharing. You're the one always locking herself in the bathroom for hours.'

'I value my privacy.'

'Yeah. But we should also spare time for our friends, shouldn't we?'

Suddenly what she was saying seemed to translate into what Leo had been saying to me that morning: that he'd missed me, even though we'd been together the whole time. 'Yeah, well,' I said. 'I s'pose you're right – it's me.'

'Well, actually, it isn't. It's all of us. Some more than others. You need your friends, yeah? Listen, I understand what you're going through, don't forget that. I've been there. Who can you trust, eh?'

'Yeah,' I said. 'Who can you?'

'But you need to trust someone,' she said, 'don't you?'

She made me think of Beccs for a moment, regretting the very limited access I'd had to the one person in the world I trusted above all others.

'There has to be someone you can trust,' Angel was saying. 'I don't tell lies.'

'So it was a set?' I said. 'Necklace and earrings?'

'You can see it was,' she said. 'It's obvious, isn't it? I've seen you looking at them. They're the same, aren't they – the earrings are the same as your necklace.'

I touched the stone.

'It'll not bring you any luck,' Angel said, noticing my hand movement, the tender touch of my fingers. 'He's just like the rest of them,' she said, 'you know that? They're all the same. This is what they do.'

'I don't believe it.'

'Why not? You can see it, can't you?'

'No. I can't. It's a coincidence. Somebody must have said it looks like a set, so everybody thinks it was. I'll ask her.'

'Oh, yeah. And what do you think she'll say? Ask him as well, why don't you? What do you think he'll say? Come off it! Use your head, girl. What is she? Look at her. She's a Ho!'

'So what is he, then?'

'He's a – he's male. That's what they do. You think you've got something, you think you've found something special –'

'And you can't stand it, can you! If I had something special, how you'd hate it, wouldn't you? I think you're jealous.'

She went quiet for a long, long while. She seemed to be steeling herself as if for a fight. I felt coiled in sprung-steel tension myself, hunched defensively in my window seat.

'Jealous?' she hissed, with the word leaking from between gritted teeth. 'You still don't get it, do you? I'm not jealous. It just makes me sick to see what he's doing to you. It makes me sick when she's so happy about it. The whole thing just makes me – what do I have to do? You want me to show you something? You want me to show you more proof?'

'What can you possibly show me?'

'Oh, I can. Don't worry about that!'

She was away again then, black angel wings flapping in my face, trailing a window-smear of dark moth powder. My eyes felt gritty and dry as my neck throbbed on a pulsating vein. I tried to lick my lips but my tongue was stuck to the roof of my mouth.

It might have been my imagination, it was impossible to tell, but I swear I saw Angel share a bitchy little slanting glance with Miranda as she passed. Miranda immediately shot a bolt of a look in my direction without the smile, but with the bitch still totally intact.

The pulse in my neck was growing harder and faster. Yes, I wanted to be shown something; I wanted more proof. More than that though, much more than that, I wanted to lash out at – I wanted revenge. Against whom? Against Miranda? Adam? Angel?

If Angel has something to show me, if she had more proof, then I'd know. And knowing, act.

And what would I do? How to wreak such revenge? I'd know, when the time came. Oh yes, I'd know what to do then, whoever they were!

# ✳✳✳ Twenty-One

'**A**MY PEPPERCORN!' – written large.

'And Car Crime' – in smaller type.

'Featuring the Static Cats' – as an additional feature, written quite small, almost as an afterthought.

The billing pleased me, for once. I was not embarrassed into modesty by the Cats appearing additionally, as my backing group. That's what they were. It made me feel better, slightly: only slightly. It was something I had over Miranda, as she swanned about, flaunting the earrings in front of me, as if to hurt me with them, as if to wreak some petty revenge for the fact that my name appeared in the biggest letters at the very top of the posters and on the T-shirts and in the press. My songs were getting airplay wherever we went. *If Ever* was doing surprisingly well. The American backers, Al Gerrard III and his team of guys, were doing an excellent job.

America, as I've said before, is such a hard market for a band to break, but we were doing pretty well. I think there was a lot more happening behind the scenes, what with Solar and PPF pulling different strings. I was lucky. We all were, but I was the luckiest. My name was the one it all hung upon. I was the one the press, TV and radio wanted to interview, although quite often we all went.

'Car Crime kicks ass!' Kaylie would always cry out.

'That's what I'd like to do to her,' Angel would hiss into my ear, always ready with a whispered comment to criticise one of the others.

The thing was, I'd so often seen her hanging on to the ears of the others – Kaylie and Miranda, Ben and Dave, even Leo – spispering away when she made out she thought nobody was watching. She was always being watched, she knew that. Once, she had said that she considered me her best friend. It made me wonder what she had said into other ears about how friendly she was with them. She was forever looking after, looking out for, getting involved in everybody else's business.

'You'd better have something good for me,' I hissed back at her as we prepared to go on stage that evening. 'It'll have to be something cast in iron, or you and me will have to have it out, Angel. You know that?'

'Why can't you trust me?' she whispered. 'I'll show you what it's like when the two of them are together, without you.'

This, coming from my 'best friend', sounded and felt like poison in my ear. What could she possibly have on Adam and Miranda? Pictures of them together? Pictures of them close together? Closer than close? Kissing? Giving each other long, lingering French kisses? Kisses like Adam gave me? Adam kissing Miranda like he kissed me, before saying those things to her, those beautiful, untrustworthy things?

My imagination was running amok. Miranda was still wearing the earrings. As far as I could remember, she'd never worn them on stage before today. Not only did she have them on, but every time she came near to me it was with a flick of the head, displaying them right in front of me. On stage that evening, that was what she was doing. I could see it. Angel could see it. Angel's face told me again and again that she had seen what I'd seen, and more.

We were doing my song, the one for which I had composed both the words and the music, *Living the Dream*:

> *So let me down again*
> *Why don't you?*
> *I thought you were a friend*
> *Why weren't you?*

I wished we weren't doing this song. The words and everything were wrong for the way I was feeling. Or particularly right for it. Either way, it felt wrong. The Cats, none of them liked the song. Why? Because it was mine, because I'd written the whole thing.

> *I needed you*
> *You weren't there.*
> *So let me down again*
> *See if I care.*

My song. My words, my melody. The Cats were against it. They were against me. Kaylie, with the vestiges of two black eyes, glared bruises at me. Miranda threw back her head. Angel, my 'best friend', looked like someone with something juicy over someone else: me!

Me, at the centre of all this catty charm, surrounded by double-speaking smiles and looks, the four of us circling round with our Cheshire grins in place but with our tails and hackles raised as if for an impending catfight.

> *I'm living it such a lot*
> *I'm giving it all I got*
> *I'm living my dream.*
> *If you think I've lost*

*I've not.*
*I can't be double-crossed*
*I'm hot.*

The tension in the air between us was more brittle and strung-out than ever. Ben and Leo and Dave were right behind us providing the backing, while we were up-front with friction enough to create a white heat dangerously close to burning us down.

*So come round here and see*
*There's nothing I can't do.*
*Who needs an enemy*
*With friends like you?*

I launched after Miranda with those words. She dodged out of my way, with a look on her face that suggested she thought I was jealous of her. Me! Jealous of her!

Angel veered into view.

*I'm living it such a lot*
*I'm giving it all I got*
*I'm living my dream.*

If this was my living dream, what would my dying nightmare possibly be like? Try to imagine it: I couldn't.

*If you think I've lost*
*I've not.*
*I can't be double-crossed*
*I'm hot.*
*I'm not what I seem*
*I'm giving it one last shot*

*One final scream.*
*I'm living the dream!*

The on-stage tension between us made for an edgy, manically energetic performance as ever. The audience was lapping us up. We were good. Whatever else was going on between us, we worked live. We took our worked-for applause together, even though we were practically ready to scratch each other's eyes out.

'You'd better have something good,' I growled at Angel under the general noise of applause. 'You'd better be able to show me something, or I might –'

What I might have done, I wasn't sure. Something, though, because if it wasn't good enough to convince me of Adam's unfaithfulness, then the treachery would be all Angel's.

'I'll show you!' she grinned, looking totally unlike a best friend to anyone or anything. 'I'll show you, then you'll know! Then you'll thank me!'

'Oh, yeah!' I said. As if I'd be thanking her, either way. As if!

'Car Crime kicks ass!' Kaylie cried through a mike.

The crowd responded.

'So does Amy Peppercorn,' I enjoined, shoving Kaylie aside. I was looking at Angel. 'So does Amy Peppercorn,' I said.

'Come on then! Come on! Let's have it!'

'I don't have it, yet.'

'What is it?'

'I can't tell you. You won't believe me.'

'When, then?'

'Soon. Tomorrow. Or the next day.'

'You're enjoying this!'

'Am I? Is that what you think?'

Yes, oh yes, that was what I thought. What was the point of claiming to be my friend, only to keep me hanging on and hanging on like this, watching me like that, while I was feeling like this. Smiling like that.

This was the worst thing: that smile. A mock-friendly stretching of the face I wished I could find a way of knocking off for her. My best friend she professed to be, while I couldn't help but hate her. And Miranda. And Kaylie, for no real reason. They were Cats, and I'd been forced into hating all of them.

And Adam?

No. Not Adam. I hadn't seen anything yet. Only earrings of the same blue as my necklace. Nothing more. So why should I doubt him?

'Beccs,' I texted, 'should I doubt him?'

Nothing came back. Nothing.

We were still travelling from town to town, gigging. The tension was building, building. Something was going to give. Our live performances were spreading like fire, like wildfire. We were hot. We were at war, attacking one another, fighting fire with fire.

Leo was afraid of getting burnt. Ben was backing away from the heat, retreating further and further into his cool. Dave was way out of it so much of the time, chasing oblivion in the bar every night, puffing strange smoke out of the open van window all day every day.

Every day we burned up the road, stuck in a stinking van,

our destination anywhere, anywhere but there, with America
winding by virtually unvisited.

> *Hurry up, hurry up*
> *We ain't got much time.*
> *I got my motor gunning*
> *like I'm doing Car Crime.*

Now we fought on stage only, dancing in one another's face
as if about to attack, about to counter-attack.

> *Tired of sittin' waitin'*
> *'S gettin' all too much.*
> *Feel like grinding thru my gears.*
> *Feel like burning my clutch.*

# ***** Twenty-Two

'**A**my, I'm sorry. You have to know.'

'Know what? Tell me now, or leave me alone!'

'I couldn't tell you before,' Angel said, glancing over her shoulder. 'It's been difficult. I've had to take a chance. This is it,' she said, reaching into one of the side pockets of her baggy combats.

The something in her hand made me freeze. She held it out to me.

'What's this?'

'Take it,' she said. 'It's hers. Quickly.'

I took the mobile phone from her. 'This? Is this it?'

'It's hers,' she said. 'It's Miranda's.'

'So?'

'So look at it. Be quick. I've got to put it back, before she misses it.'

'Look at it?' I said, turning it over and over in my hand. 'What of it?'

'No,' she said, 'come here.' She took the phone from me and went into its address book. Under A. Straight away. A.

I knew what it stood for. Straight away. A. The number came up.

She had that look in her eyes. That look!

It was that number. It was the mobile number I had in my phone, stored against Adam's name. That number!

That look in her eyes!

That number appearing under his name on her mobile phone.

'Now you know what this means,' Angel said. 'Now you understand, don't you?'

'Oh, yes,' I said. 'I know what this means. I understand, don't you worry. I understand all right!'

We were approaching the last show of the tour. Adam had promised to be there. Angel was looking at me like the angel of doom. The look on her face was an I-told-you-so expression. I returned her looks with my own expression of hardening determination. I know exactly what this meant and how to deal with it.

Nobody was speaking to anybody else. There was nothing left to say. There never is, when so many insults and insinuations have been thrown about, spurred on by so many bad feelings. It's practically impossible, I had come to realise, for so many people to live in each other's pockets for weeks on end without learning how to severely despise one another. It was bound to happen, however friendly we were at the outset. But this had got so bad, much worse than it should have. There were too many wrong things going on between us just to leave us with an honest dislike for each other. There was hatred here, fired by jealousy.

Jealousy. How it gnawed at the lower gut, like a rat eating away at love, replacing every feeling for good with wanting, needing, despairing after revenge. That's what it wants, jealousy; it wants some kind of revenge, some kind of purposeful, destructive, rodent action, or it can never rest. And then it never rests. It's always there, locked up in a memory, a feeling brought about by a tune, a smell, the sound of a piece of music. With remembrance of place and time, will come that dreadful vengeance, that overwhelming desire to do damage.

I knew about jealousy now. I recognised it. I understood.

# ⭐⭐⭐ Twenty-Three

*So let me down again*
*Why don't you?*
*I thought you were a friend*
*Why weren't you?*

Adam was there with Pierre. They had timed their arrival to be able to watch us performing. I spotted Adam at the back of the stage in the wings, behind me to my left. I looked round at him.

*I needed you*
*You weren't there.*
*So let me down again*
*See if I care.*

Angel spotted him. So did Miranda. She was still wearing the earrings. Spotting Adam, she seemed to throw back her head, shaking the bright blue stones hanging from her ears.

*If you think I've lost*
*I've not.*
*I can't be double-crossed*
*I'm hot.*

I sang my words. 'I can't be double-crossed.' Angel was

looking at me. Angel Iago. Iago, the angel of envy. Adam's name and that number had been programmed into Miranda's phone.

*I can't be double-crossed*
*I'm hot.*

As I moved towards Adam where he stood watching with Pierre, Angel watched over us: her excited, animated face all part of the stage act, all part of her performance. She watched us as I sang, as I moved with deliberation towards where Adam waited. I knew now what it all meant. I knew what to do about it.

*I'm living it such a lot.*

As I sang, as I moved, as Adam awaited his fate, I glanced back at Angel.

*I'm giving it all I got.*

And she watched me, willing me on, standing behind me, dancing behind me, urging me to act.

*I'm living my dream!*

Angel watched as I reached out and took Adam by the hand, drawing him onto the stage. Her animated eyes sparkled, watching someone about to be slapped and publicly humiliated.

*I'm living the dream!*

And I kissed him. As she watched. Witnessed by our audience, by the other Cats, by Ben, Leo, Dave. By Pierre. For Adam. Not against him. Not that.

For I knew. I knew what it all meant. And I knew exactly what to do about it.

*If you think I've lost*
*I've not.*
*I can't be double-crossed*
*I'm hot.*
*I'm not what I seem*
*I'm giving it one last shot*
*One final scream.*
*I'm living the dream!*

# ✦✦✦ Twenty-Four

**A**dam gave me smiles: that was what I could say, quite accurately, about Adam's smiles for me. He gave them, like a gift, every time. The smile was in his eyes, even when he wasn't actually smiling. 'You will have to come back again,' he'd said. 'You have done well in America. You have started a fan base, I think. It is a good beginning.'

'Yes,' I had agreed. 'It's a good beginning. I like beginnings. I like the way they come out of endings. That's how it is for me, so often. One thing ends, another begins.'

'Not for the Static Cats, maybe,' Adam said.

'No,' I said, 'maybe not.'

The Cats had pulled themselves to pieces. I had helped, I suppose, although I couldn't help it. 'You should have checked that number,' I had said to Angel Iago, in front of the other Cats, in front of Ben and Adam.

Her face looked slapped. Adam's wasn't.

I got out my mobile phone, went into the address book and tapped in an A. 'Adam' came up immediately, with a mobile number. I pressed dial. 'Listen,' I said to Angel, handing her the phone.

She listened. I couldn't hear what she heard, but I knew exactly what it was going to say: 'Hello, you've reached Amy. I'm not available at the moment, but . . .'

I watched her slapped face listening, her eyes looking up at me. 'You should have checked the number,' I said, 'before you copied it into Miranda's phone.'

'What?' Miranda said. 'What happened?'

'That's my number,' I said. I had put my number against Adam's name when I found out Ray Ray was interfering with my phone and with my private life. Adam's mobile number was stored against something else. 'And Miranda's never called my number, have you?'

'No! Why?'

'I don't know what you're talking about,' Angel tried to say. Her eyes said something else, something very different.

Miranda was pressing buttons on her phone.

'Try A,' I said.

'What's this?' she said.

'Well, what did you expect her to say?' Angel said, without looking at Miranda. She wasn't looking at anything but me, straight at me, as if I'd just struck her.

'Lapis lazuli,' I said.

'What?' said Miranda.

'Lapis lazuli. That's what I have Adam's number stored against. It's what your earrings are made of, Miranda.'

'What? My earrings?'

'Like my necklace. You must have noticed?'

'Yeah. I just liked the blue.'

'So did Angel, didn't you, Angel? Was she there when you bought them, Miranda?'

'Course I wasn't!'

'I dunno. Yeah. You were. You liked them. No, you saw them first.'

'You don't know what you're talking about,' said Angel as if she was speaking to Miranda, but still looking at me.

'Then where did those rumours come from?' I said.

'What rumours?' Miranda said.

'Angel said –' Kaylie tried to say, to join in the fun.

'I never said anything! You don't know what you're talking about! You all make me sick!' Angel screamed. 'Do you know that? You all make me sick. I'm glad this stupid tour's over. Do you know what? So are the Cats – so over! Because I've got a recording contract and it's just –'

'Who with?' the girls wanted to know.

'Solar, who else? Solar Records! Yeah! A recording contract, a real one, for Angel Iago, and no stupid Cats. Get it? Get it?'

Yeah, we got it. I did, certainly.

Courtney Schaeffer's recording contract had come to an end. My old pop-rival's record company was not interested in re-signing her. 'Have you heard about Courtney?' Angel Iago said to me, with a Cat-scratch on her left cheek. Ben and Dave had had to pull the other Cats apart to stop them from tearing Angel's wings off. Leo had screamed from the other side of the room as Kaylie and Miranda had gone for her, tooth and claw. It was the end of the tour, tooth and claw, a scream, and there was the end to it.

But the end had come at the end, if you follow my meaning. I mean, it was over. The fighting without pillows was about to become very real, as Angel's face attested as she came over later to speak to me. 'Courtney Schaeffer,' she said. The red mark down her cheek glowed through her make-up. She was hurt, but it didn't show up entirely, not the way she covered everything with foundation and false friendship.

'I heard,' I said. 'Courtney's recording contract is finished. They're not re-signing her.'

'No,' Angel said, 'but Ray is.'

'Ray is?'

'She's with Solar now, too,' she said, trying to smile, wincing for a moment against the pain in her face. 'So we're all with Solar now,' she cringed. 'You and me and Courtney, all together.'

And I saw through her smile to the roots of Ray Ray's distorted sense of humour. Divide and Conquer – that was Ray's motto. Angel had a recording contract with Solar too. She was jealous. So was Ray. She smiled like he did, insincerely through the cracks in her face. I didn't know if Ray was already behind Angel, whether or not she had been representing his interests throughout the tour, and I didn't care. She and Courtney and Ray and anybody else could gang up against me, trying to get me down or set me up or manipulate or manage me down to my very thought-processes – however overwhelmed I felt, being the subject of their many manipulations, I was all right, because I was not included in the jealousy that drives, that embitters and eats away at the people, whoever they were, in Ray's green-gilled gang. I was all right. So was Adam. We were fine!

# ✦✦✦ Twenty-Five

This was how I was feeling on my way to Beccs' on that bright, autumn Saturday morning: I felt like a winner, walking on the aircushion of the pavements I knew so well from the childhood I'd shared with my best friend. Walking round to see Beccs, after everything that had happened, I couldn't help but feel that I had grown. I had experience. It was good. Everything looked great. I couldn't wait to tell Beccs all about it. It felt like such a long time since I'd seen my friend. I had so much to tell her.

I was going to tell her about what Angel had tried to do to Adam and me, but in so saying would tell of Adam himself, where there was so much to say, because he was so unusual. As Adam said, it is beautiful to be unusual, so why not enjoy it, why not revel in being different? Which is what I was too, I felt. Adam helped me celebrate what I was. 'Beccs,' I was looking forward to saying to her, 'he is beautiful. Through all the cause I had to doubt him, I never seriously doubted him. Even when it made sense to suspect, I felt something other than doubt. Something else, I felt. You know, something else.'

So the end had come. Of the tour, that is. We finished in the suburb high schools of San Francisco, Amy P, the car criminals, a scattering of cats. It was over.

And yet it had truly begun: Adam and I, together, in that beautiful city. No doubt. Adam and me: with nothing in between us, nothing to separate us. It felt wonderful. I felt beautiful. With the world at my feet! London! Berlin! Paris! San Francisco! They knew of me, they knew me in all these places. Even Ray Ray couldn't interfere with me now.

Beccs! Oh Beccs, how I'd missed her. How I was magnified, living large, bubbling over with all I had to tell her. We'd missed so much of each other while I'd been away. It was time to catch up.

That walk to my friend's house was so wonderful, with the pavements under my feet glittering with gold. I hadn't even told her I was home yet. It was going to be such a surprise. I felt great. The people passing knew me. They said hello as I went by. I loved them. Everything was so good, nothing could have brought me down. Or so I thought.

So I was thinking as I knocked on the door that morning, as the door opened and Beccs' mum looked at me, smiling there almost as if she didn't recognise me. Perfect strangers everywhere said hello as I passed. Beccs' mum looked at me as perfect strangers do to perfect strangers.

'Hello, Mrs Bradley,' I sang out. The sun was shining. Birds behind me were singing like cats, a natural band providing the backing track to my happiness.

'Oh,' Mrs Bradley said, not looking so good, 'hello, Amy. Was Rebecca expecting you this morning?'

'No,' I smiled, although she did not, 'I wanted to surprise her.'

'Oh,' Mrs Bradley said again.

This was the first time ever that Mrs Bradley had asked me if Beccs was expecting me. Beccs didn't have to expect a call from me. What, was I supposed to make an appointment or something? 'Is something wrong, Mrs Bradley?'

For a moment, Beccs' mum looked as if she was about to say something. 'She's in her room,' she said. She might have been saying something else, from the way she sounded. 'You'd better go up.'

'Look at what you've done,' Leo had been saying to me.

'What have I done?'

'You've done it all,' he said, 'without me.'

'But you were there, with us, the whole time.'

'Was I? Lovely, I was along for the ride. You don't need me any more.'

'Leo, I –'

'No, sweet, don't think I'm going away. You'll never be rid of me now.'

'I'm glad.'

'But you don't actually need me. Look at what you've done. It's you. Look at you. All grown up.'

I felt like crying. Leo was lovely. But he was right: I'd done so much, achieved so much. I was in love. Yes, I was. In love. I was sure. Now I knew. I cried. I was happy. I stopped crying. I was powerful.

I was flying up the stairs in Beccs' house, bursting with love and vitality, desperate to let my friend, my best ever friend, in on it all, on all my emotions and secrets and secret emotions. Her mum watched me bounding up two steps at a time until I disappeared onto the landing, and no doubt listened as I thumped through Beccs' bedroom door about to burst with –

Oh no!

'Oh, no,' I said.

I was in love. All my love came welling up as she turned from the books on her piled high little worktable, as she looked up at me, fumbling to take off her earphones.

'Beccs,' I said.
She smiled.
I had never – such –
'Oh, Beccs!'
Still she smiled.
Then she tried to get up.

# ✳✳✳ Twenty-Six

**A**ll that stuff, all my stuff, the world whirling round me, fell away as she stumbled. Running up the stairs I had felt fantastic. It now suddenly felt as if I'd run up too furiously, forcing my way in only to be smacked in the face by a full stop.

Beccs had been studying, I think, or at least looking at her books as I banged and barged in on her. Seeing me suddenly in her bedroom doorway, Beccs turned and tried to stand. She seemed to stumble, almost fall. There was an unfamiliar concentration on her face as she consciously corrected the tilting of her body. She smiled.

'Beccs! What's . . . happened?'

Still she smiled. But the skin seemed stretched across her face, her cheeks drawn in and sallow, her eyes dark-ringed and sunken.

Beccs was a football player. But her legs no longer looked as if she was good at kicking a ball. She was thinner: far, far thinner than I had ever seen her. Ever. Thinner than – thinner than thin should ever have been on a thick-set and strong sturdy body like hers.

'Oh, Beccs!'

But still the smile never departed her stretched-tight lips. The truth in her eyes couldn't break that smile of hers. She was determined not to give in. Of everything I could detect in her, it was her sheer will to win that was most evident, in her eyes and in her strong but slanted stance.

She didn't move any closer to me. 'I hurt my leg,' she said. When she moved, just shifting position, I could see the hurt of her leg in her face.

'When?' I said.

'Weeks ago.'

'Weeks?'

'Weeks and weeks. Just after our birthday party.'

'But why isn't it –'

'It isn't getting any better.'

We stood looking at each other. Looking and looking at each other. Oh, she could hide the tears out of her eyes, but not the fear. That she could not hide, because I was feeling it for her, and showing every bit of it.

'Please don't,' she whispered.

But I couldn't help it. I was afraid. I was so afraid.

'I hurt my leg,' she said, 'playing football. It didn't get any better. Then I caught a cold. That got worse. It just got worse and worse. I had to go on strong antibiotics. I'm still on them. It hasn't gone. I can't seem to get better.'

'But why? What is it? What's going on?'

'I don't know. I've been having tests. There's something wrong with my immune system. It doesn't seem to be working properly. Or it's working the wrong way. It's kind of got confused, so it's starting to attack all the wrong things.'

'The wrong things?'

'Like – as if it doesn't like me. As if my own immune system thinks I'm the enemy. It thinks I'm a virus or something. Isn't that stupid?'

221

\*\*\*

'But why didn't you tell me?'

She looked away. 'Would you have told me?'

'Yes!'

'No, you wouldn't. If I'd been away concentrating on an important tour, doing the things you've been doing, would you have bothered me with it?'

'Yes!'

'No. You wouldn't.'

'It doesn't matter. It's too important. It's just too important. Tell me! Don't do this to me, Beccs. I mean it. Don't you dare.'

# **Twenty-Seven**

'It could be leukaemia,' she said.

She said it as if it was any old thing. I tried to treat it in the same way. I failed. It wasn't any old thing. It just wasn't!

# ✱✱✱ Twenty-Eight

'It was Angel Iago,' I said.

'The jealous cow!'

'Yes. But she's damaged, mixed up. She's been hurt.'

'So? Anyone can find excuses. There are no excuses.'

'Anyway, she's no match for you.'

'No,' I said, trying to sound as positive and as powerful as I had been feeling before I'd seen my best friend like this.

'Not even with Courtney,' Beccs said, smiling. Her eyes glinted, telling of her happiness.

Oh, if she'd only been sad, or mad, it would not have been half as heartbreaking. My breath was going as I looked into the happy gladness she held for me in her eyes. She was so brave, so very, very brave. She made me feel like a coward because of all my fear.

'No,' she said, without my having to say anything, 'I'm frightened too.'

To see her saying this, with that smile on her face, with that look of happiness in her eyes, was too much to bear. I couldn't stand it. 'No,' I said, breaking with it, letting go, 'no Beccs. Not this. Not you. Oh, God, I'm so selfish. So, so bloody selfish!'

*⋆*⋆

'You're part of my reason,' I said, when I had finally collected my emotions sufficiently enough to speak. 'You're part of the reason I do what I do. I want to be successful so that I can share it with you. I want you to do the same for me.'

'And I shall.'

'Because if you – no, you shall. Nothing's going to stop you. Nothing!'

'Nothing!' she repeated. 'Nor you. Nothing's going to stop us!'

'Nothing!' I chanted.

No, nothing. Ray Ray, Jagdish Mistri, Angel Iago, leukaemia – nothing!

'We're unstoppable!' Beccs cried, raising a fist into the air. She stood up, correcting the tilt given to her body by one bent leg. 'Nothing can stop us!'

'Nothing!' I cried, leaping up, fisting the air with her. 'You and me! I don't care!'

'Neither do I! Neither do I!'

# ✵ Twenty-Nine

**W**e were laughing. Beccs' mum came in with a tray for us. 'That's better,' she said, smiling at our laughter. 'That's more like it.'

I had been telling Beccs about Adam. 'I love him already,' she had said, just before her mum appeared. We laughed.

'That's more like my daughter,' Mrs Bradley said. She looked at me with kind and caring eyes.

'And that's just like my friend,' I said, holding Beccs' hand.

'And we don't care,' Beccs said.

Mrs Bradley's face showed a moment of panic, as if not caring meant giving in.

'We don't care,' I said, 'because nothing can stop us. We're too strong, Mrs Bradley.'

The changing expression of Beccs' mum's face, the tightness, the firmness, the permanence of Beccs' hand-hold confirmed it for me, for us all: we were unstoppable.

You just watch. There's nothing we can't do, me and my friend, my friend and me. If you could have seen us then, at that moment, you'd have been as convinced of us as we ourselves were, as Mrs Bradley was. We were invincible together.

I was in love.

So was Beccs.

In love with life.

That was the important thing.
That is the important thing!
You just watch!

*Look out for . . .*

## Amy Peppercorn: Starry-eyed and Screaming

Amy has a lot to scream about. Her best friend Beccs is being lured away by that hateful boy beacon, Kirsty. School sucks. Her family is impossible to live with.

Then – although she *so* didn't mean to – she falls under the spell of the cool, irresistible Ben and joins his band. Everything changes.

Because Amy's scream is her fortune. She's going to be a pop sensation and she's on her way.

Stardom has its price – how much will Amy pay?

# Amy Peppercorn: Living the Dream

Amy is an overnight sensation. She is top of the pops.

Amy's living the dream – and she's carrying the guilt. Geoff is dead. Ben is on remand. She's lost best friend Beccs and even Mum seems out of reach.

On tour, in the midst of glamour and fame, starry performances and screaming crowds, Amy's never been so utterly lonely.

Cue the mysterious Jag Mistri – he seems so perfect, a friend who can make the dream last for ever . . .

# Amy Peppercorn: Beyond the Stars

Amy Peppercorn was once an ordinary girl with a big voice. Now she's a star!

She's conquered the UK, and now she's off to Paris. There she meets the dark-eyed singer Adam Bede, who knows all her songs, and wants to get to know her a lot better.

Back home, Ben, the boy who once seemed so irresistible, is all too present in the recording studio, wrestling with his memories and his conscience.

And then the headlines explode. Amy's life is laid out for all to see. Truth or lies – does it matter?

As Amy heads off to wow the USA, the headlines haunt her and hunt her down. And her dream life begins to flicker . . .